THE KEEPER OF SECRETS
BOOK 1

WRITTEN BY KERRI HILL

First published in paperback in Australia
by EQUESTRIAN COUNTRY PUBLISHING
November 2023

Photography and Graphic Design by Kerri Hill
Book Design by Kerri Hill
Artwork of Santiago on the cover by Samantha Pearce
Santiago Name Design by Troy Sizer
Design on page six by Dorota Kudyba

ENTERTAINMENT

Amurath Santiago FB page @amurathSantiago
Vist our website to keep up to date
www.santiagoentertainment.com.au

All Copyright © belongs to Kerri Hill
All moral rights of Kerri Hill have been asserted.

ISBN - 978-0-646-84041-3

All rights reserved.
This book or any portion thereof may not be reproduced or transmitted in any form or by any means,
electronic or mechanical, including photocopying, recording, storage in an information retrieval system,
or otherwise without the prior written permission of the publishers, unless specifically permitted under
the Australian Copyright Act 1968 as amended.

Conditions of Sale
This book is sold subject to the condition, that it shall not, by way of trade or otherwise, be lent, re-sold,
hired out or otherwise circulated without the publishers prior consent in any form, binding or cover
other than that in which it it published and without a similar condition including this condition being
imposed on the subsequent purchaser.

Santiago

BASED ON THE TRUE-LIFE ADVENTURES OF AN ARABIAN HORSE NAMED

AMURATH SANTIAGO

WRITTEN BY KERRI HILL

CONTENTS

Santiago

THE KEEPER OF SECRETS

I dedicate this book to all those who were ever told - or ever felt - that they weren't good enough. Or who were told they couldn't or shouldn't follow their heart. This book is for you. May you always persevere and rise above the doubters. And may you boldly overcome your own self-doubt. This book is for all the dreamers who need to find the courage to embark on their own, extraordinary journey.

Kerri Hill

KERRI WITH SANTIAGO
SCOTTSDALE ARIZONA

ABOUT THE AUTHOR

I may be a first-time author, but storytelling and crafting imaginative concepts have always been ingrained in my soul. Creativity and the art of storytelling are my life passions. So I'm truly excited to embark on this new journey as an author.

As I look back on my life so far, I see a journey defined by challenging obstacles but also filled with personal triumphs. My own story begins in a small town during the 80s, at a time when little was known about dyslexia or ADHD. I was a child who struggled in school and particularly with reading and writing. The words on the page seemed to dance rather than talk. Their true meaning often eluded my grasp. But amid these challenges, I always found solace in art. And I soon discovered that my imagination knew no bounds.

But it wasn't until I was in my mid 20's that the puzzling pieces of my life finally began to fit together. A professional diagnosis of dyslexia and ADHD shed new light on the reasons behind my lifelong struggles. It was a revelation that brought so much clarity to my past.

During my early years, although it was evident that I possessed potential and intelligence, I was often labeled as 'not trying hard enough'. Or as lazy and 'simply not measuring up.' I carried the weight of these judgments into my teenage years and they only further fuelled my frustration.

So, at the tender age of 15, I made the bold decision to leave school behind and pursue my passion for horse riding. I committed to becoming a professional equestrian and the glorious world of horses became my refuge. But life often has a way of, unexpectedly, changing our course.

At the age of 16, my world took a drastic turn, when a horse riding accident left me permanently paralysed and confined to a wheelchair. I spent a gruelling ten months in the hospital and celebrated my 17th birthday undergoing intensive rehabilitation. Life had handed me another unexpected challenge and yet I chose to embrace it with resilience.

So please don't feel sorry for me. I have lived an extraordinary life. My life journey continued to unfold after my accident, eventually leading me to a career in makeup and special effects for the international film and television industry. I relocated to America, where I found myself working alongside some of Hollywood's brightest stars. I was soon living a life of adventure and excitement, albeit from the vantage point of my (vibrant pink) wheelchair.

Instead of viewing my dyslexia and ADHD as disabilities, I found a way to transform them into superpowers.

My insatiable passion for life became my driving force. I also discovered that if something didn't captivate me, I would lose interest quickly. When I read or wrote, it had to be not just engaging but deeply meaningful to me. And that's how Santiago, my beloved Arabian horse, became the inspiration for this story.

However, life continued to present its share of obstacles. The sudden loss of my beloved Santiago, in 2018, cast such a shadow of grief over my work that progress on this project was stalled for nearly three years. It was a period of mourning, healing and reflection. But even during this difficult time, I never gave up on my dream.

So after a decade of twists and turns, you are now reading the introduction to Santiago; the Keeper of Secrets. It has taken years of soul-searching, setbacks and reinventions to reach this point. I tried collaborating with others to bring this story to life, but the universe seemed to always be conspiring to lead me back to writing this book myself. It was a daunting challenge. But it was also a journey I believe I was always destined to embark upon.

In this book, I will share the story of my real family's journey to Australia - and the adventures that unfolded - along with the profound connection I shared with Santiago throughout.

It is a true tale of resilience and transformation. A story about turning adversity into an opportunity - with a tantalising touch of fantasy thrown in!

I also want to extend my heartfelt gratitude to those friends who have supported me as I have undertaken this incredible journey.

To Kelly Koolstra-Aplin, Rebecca Booth, Troy Galvin and Sophie Campbell. Your unwavering belief in me - even when I lacked the confidence within myself - made all the difference. You are not just friends; you are my village and my support system. I couldn't have done this without you!

The path to this book has been long and winding. It has been a journey filled with moments of self-doubt and challenges that regularly threatened to deter me. Yet, here we are…at the beginning of a brand new chapter in my life. It is a chapter that celebrates the strength of the human spirit and the beauty of embracing our own uniqueness.

I also hope that sharing my story serves as an inspiration for all of you to embark on your own journeys with courage, strength and unwavering self-belief. If I can overcome the odds and pursue my dreams, so can each and every one of you.

I believe the story of my life is a personal testament to the incredible resilience of the human spirit and the power of believing in oneself.

DREAM BIG

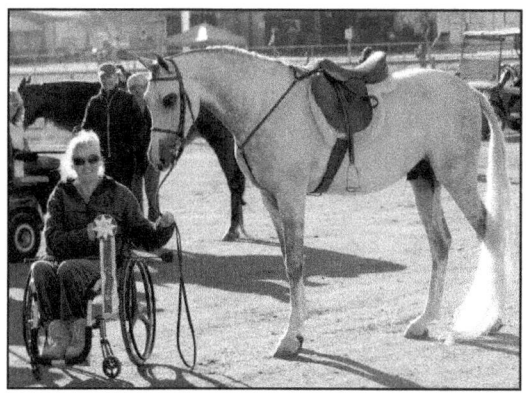

KERRI WITH SANTIAGO AT ONE OF HIS FIRST SHOWS, SCOTTSDALE ARIZONA USA

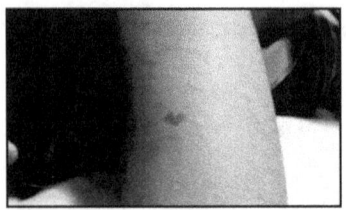

Sometimes, life weaves its own enchanting magic that resembles a fairy tale, yet it's undeniably real. Santiago and Addison each bear perfect heart-shaped markings, Santiago on his head, and Addison on her arm.

Addison and Ashley Price riding Santiago together - "Double dinking"

SANTIAGO & ADDISON

Addison and Santiago achieved a remarkable feat in 2013, by winning the title of Australian National Champion in their Youth class. Addison had only just turned seven years old and this was her first time ever showing in halter.

The competition was fierce, with some of Australia's top youth handlers and horses competing for the prestigious title. But Santiago and Addison managed to stand out, mainly because of the striking size difference between them. Memorably, Santiago displayed an exwceptional level of gentleness in every step he took that day, making Addison's victory even more remarkable. This 'moment in time' only reaffirmed my love of the Arabian breed and the incredible intuition and connection they share with their handlers.

Santiago consistently demonstrated his gentle nature to the world, especially when interacting with me in my wheelchair. He could also showcase his fiery and spirited side, whenever a bit more 'spark' was required. Santiago truly embodied the essence of a 'true gentleman'.

More photos of Santiago and his real life adventures are featured in the back of this book.

Photos on this page by Samantha Taylor

13

THE KEEPER OF SECRETS
BOOK 1

Have you ever harboured a secret so big that your whole life revolves around it? Well, let me spill the tea, because I've got one that's been locked up tighter than a safe at Fort Knox. Only a select few are privy to this classified information, including my brother, Ethan, and my new best friend, Ali. They kinda stumbled onto this secret, and now we're this epic super-secret squad, bound by an unbreakable oath to protect it at all costs.

Now, let me introduce you to the bad guys—the notorious ghost pirates. These scallywags are on a mission, a treasure hunt like no other. Their target? My closely guarded secret, all in a mad scramble to get their grubby mitts on this enchanted amulet that's basically the stuff of legends. What's more, this amulet was concealed by none other than the mermaids themselves, to keep it safe from these ghost pirates.

But here's the twist you won't see coming—we've banded together, forming an unstoppable alliance with the mermaids. Yep, you heard that right. It's going to be a showdown that's epic, and we're determined to put an end to these ghost pirates' wicked plans. Together, we're ready to make sure they walk the plank, or, you know, whatever mermaids do to deal with ghost pirates. It's a battle of wits, magic, and courage, and we're in it to win!

But before we delve further into this riveting narrative, let's hit the brakes and rewind to where this adventure all began. The tricky part is, I'm not really sure where the story even begins. This is one epic tale with twists and turns that'll make your head spin. And trust me, folks, this story's got more layers than an onion on steroids. To truly tell this tale, it will require more than one volume; you are currently immersed in the first instalment.

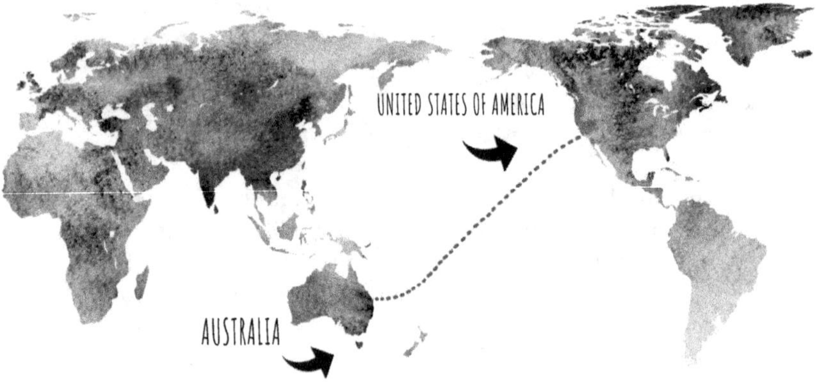

UNITED STATES OF AMERICA

AUSTRALIA

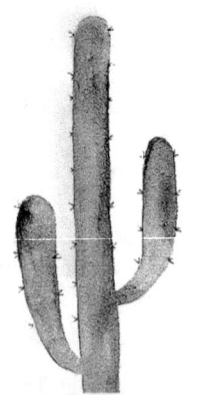

CHAPTER ONE
THE BIG MOVE

I'm Addison Steel, a typical 14-year-old, originally from the scorching desert of Scottsdale, Arizona, USA. However, a few months back, my family decides to shake things up in a big way. We pack our bags, leave the cacti behind, and land in the super-pretty coastal town of Port Cooper, in Queensland, Australia.

Now, the reason for this epic migration isn't your run-of-the-mill move. It all goes back to my mom's family legacy. You see, my mom's Aunt Sally, who owned the town's historic pub called The Haunted Lilly, passed away. And guess what? My mom inherits the whole shebang, including the pub. It's like a family tradition that's been passed down from one generation of women to the next, almost like a mystical torch that gets handed over.

The Haunted Lilly has its own distinct identity within Port Cooper, tracing its roots back to the town's inception over a century ago. Once the favoured gathering place for sailors, fishermen, and even the pirates, it remains an interesting fixture in the community's history. While time may have weathered her appearance, the pub's interior serves as a living testament, like a local museum of some kind with nostalgia of the old days.

The pub's timeworn walls are adorned with intriguing paintings that weave tales of pirates, ancient seafaring vessels, and even mermaids. When you step into the pub, your eyes are immediately drawn to a grand, wooden mermaid sculpture at the entrance that serves as a welcoming sentinel, evoking the essence of a long-past age. It's as if the very soul of maritime history is still alive within these hallowed walls.

The backstory gets even more intriguing when you learn that my mom's parents tragically died in a car accident when she was just five years old. She was raised by her Aunt Sally and Uncle Jerry, who took her in after the accident and raised her at The Haunted Lilly. this was until my mom decided to venture out of Port Cooper to chase her dreams as a makeup and special effects artist in Hollywood, California, USA. It was there that she met my dad, Grant Steel, who happened to be a set builder for films and TV. It's like a real-life love story. Their love story unfolded, culminating in the birth of my older brother, Ethan, who's 17, and later, yours truly.

My mom is undeniably one of the most resilient people I know. She had this insane horse-riding accident when she was just 16, during a cross-country event in the pouring rain. Her horse straight-up slipped and crashed her into a jump, and she ended up breaking her back and a bunch of other stuff. That accident put her in a wheelchair forever, but honestly, I've never known her any different.

My mom is a total legend. She's never once pulled the "pity me" routine or used her wheelchair as an excuse to be lazy. No way. She's done some seriously wild things that most people only dream about. For instance, when she was just 21, she packed her bags and hopped on a plane to America to chase her dreams in Hollywood. She's always been my role model for her incredible courage and determination.

We share a profound obsession for horses, a love that runs deep in our veins. When we lived in Arizona, we showed and rode Arabian horses together. But when we moved to Australia, we had to leave our two horses with my dad's folks on their ranch in Scottsdale. They're all about Arabians, too, so we know our horses are in good hands. When we FaceTime my grandparents, they take the phone to our horses, which might sound somewhat silly, but we love it, and our horses go nuts when they hear our voices and do a big loud neigh. Only another horse lover would appreciate why we're so crazy about our horses and find so much peace and pleasure spending time with them.

Regrettably, my dad and my brother fail to comprehend our fervour for horses. They're not into horses like me and my mom. They call it an obsession, rather than a hobby. And honestly, I have to agree with them. It's more than just a hobby; it's a whole way of life. I'm so grateful I get to share this "obsession" with my mom. She still rides and knows everything about horses. She's like my go-to guru when it comes to anything horse-related. She's my rock, my best friend and my horse bible, all rolled into one.

Allow me to introduce you to my brother and my father! They're a big part of this story, and honestly, all the crazy magical stuff we've been through has brought us even closer as a family. They're like this dynamic duo when it comes to music. It's not just a hobby for them; it's a full-on obsession, like the horses are for me and my mom. But hey, we all need our passions, right? I'm totally cool with them having their own thing. They're also into building stuff, which is pretty rad. You should've seen their faces when they checked out the state of The Haunted Lilly. It needs a lot of work and my dad and my brother smiled at each other and we just knew by the look on their faces they wanted to get started on the renovations as soon as they could secure the necessary tools.

Currently, they're toying with the idea of more than just a facelift for the old lady—they want to turn the ballroom into a rocking concert venue. They're planning on booking some killer bands to breathe new life into the place and maybe rake in some moolah. It's got me all pumped, and I'm stoked to see where it goes! Life kind of went off the rails when all the magical mayhem started, but that's alright, there's always time to get back on track.

Life was pretty normal before all this craziness. A new town, a new school, new riding stables—you know the deal. I was just trying to make friends and blend in. Little did I know, things were about to get seriously wild. Like, I'm talking fairy tales and magic kind of wild. I used to be a skeptic, but now I'm all in. I'm part of the magic now, and it's changed everything.

I've witnessed things that'll leave you in awe, and I've got all the juicy details. From mysterious artefacts to encounters with creatures right out of legends—it's all a part of my life now. And you're about to embark on a wild journey as I spill the beans. But remember, this isn't some made-up story; this is my real-life adventure. So, find a cosy spot, because we're diving headfirst into a world where magic and reality collide.

Now, let me introduce you to Santiago. This horse is truly exceptional. You can't even fathom how truly extraordinary he is. It all began with him. He's not just a part of the magic; he is the embodiment of magic itself. I still remember the first time I saw Santiago. It was a bright sunny morning my mom drove us to the local riding school. Remarkably, it was the same stable where she used to ride when she was younger, even before her accident. She was stoked to take me to the riding school, to show me where she grew up and for us to look into getting back to riding horses now that we'd moved.

You won't believe what happened when we turned into the driveway of the riding school?! There was this drop-dead gorgeous grey Arabian horse, and he legit popped his head up, like he was welcoming us or something. I couldn't contain my excitement, and I practically yelled at my mom:

"WOW, mom look! It's an Arabian! He's absolutely beautiful. I wonder who owns him?"

My mom just gave me this knowing smile that she does and said, "Well, I guess we're about to find out."

But seriously, this horse was something else. As we drove down the driveway, he began to canter alongside the fence, matching the speed of our car. It was like he was putting on a show just for us. I couldn't tear my eyes away from him. He was truly magnificent.

Finally, we pulled into the parking lot near the stables, and I was all ready to dash over and give that horse some loving pats and scratches. But first things first, my mom needed her wheelchair out of the back of the SUV. Priorities, you know?

I was so eager to give that stunning Arabian a pat, but my mom, being the responsible one, reminded me that we should probably introduce ourselves first and ask permission before we go all-in with the petting. She had a point, and I didn't want to start off on the wrong hoof, you know?

The stables had a cool calm vibe to them, a bit different from what I was used to back in the U.S. I was low-key, hoping to make some new friends who share our passion for horses. I mean, we'd only been in town for a week, and I was seriously craving some horsey interactions and as well as some new pals.

As my mom was chatting it up with the head instructors, I couldn't resist the temptation to start patting the nearby horses. Their inquisitive heads poking out of their stable doors, like they were curious about this new human in the stable. Oh boy, how much I'd missed the smell of horses and touching their soft velvet muzzles.

And then I came across this stunning palomino, and her head was just begging for some pats. So, I started stroking her and softly whispered, "So what's your name, pretty one?"

Suddenly, I hear this faint voice coming from behind the stable door, saying, "Her name is Candy," and a girl emerged, previously kneeling down to put hoof oil on her horse's feet. She had the biggest smile on her face and it felt so welcoming.

I respond with, "Hi, Candy and you're…?"

The girl stood up and replied, "Oh hey, I'm Ali. Candy's my horse. Her show name is Diamond Road Candy Crush, but Candy for short and I keep her here at the riding school. My dad's a fisherman, and we live on the pier, so I can't really keep Candy there, can I?"

I was somewhat taken aback by how chatty Ali was, but there was something about her warm and friendly nature that made me realise right away that we were destined to be good friends. Ali asked me my name and if I had my own horse. I had to sadly admit:

"We just moved here like a week ago from America, and I'm seriously missing having my own horse. We came to the stables to check things out and see about riding again. I was hoping I can make some new friends because I literally don't know anyone here yet. Oh and I'm Addison, Addy for short."

Ali's response was like music to my ears. She cheerfully squealed, "YES! I'd love to be your friend and show you around the stables and around town. And you're totally welcome to ride Candy, if you want! Oh, and by the way, I love your accent."

I couldn't help but break into a big smile, even though I had totally forgotten about my accent and the fact that I was in a totally new country. It was clear that this friendship was kicking off to an awesome start and I was excited for the future.

I was super curious about that beautiful grey Arabian out in the paddock near the car park. So, I asked Ali about him, and she was quick to spill the beans. "Turns out, he's a total mystery. He just showed up around a week ago, all on his own, without an owner or anything.

Just trotted up the driveway and chose that exact paddock and won't let anyone get close to him. The instructors are stumped about what to do with him."

I shared with Ali how he had cantered up the driveway as we pulled in, and she couldn't contain her excitement. She squealed again and said, "OMG, how cool is that? Wow... He really is a mystery, isn't he? I could tell that Ali was the type to get excited about the smallest things, and honestly, I liked her energy. I was really looking forward to getting to know her and Candy more.

I glanced over and noticed a group of girls at the other end of the stable, all eyeing us and snickering. I asked Ali, "Who are those girls?"

Ali gave me the lowdown, "Oh, that's the mean girls club. The ringleader is Karin, and let's just say she's not the nicest person around here. She's a bit of a bully, you know? The rest of the girls, well, they're her 'crew', I guess you can call them. My advice? Keep your distance from them."

I took her advice to heart. Drama and mean girls weren't what I was here for. I just wanted to enjoy the company of horses and have fun while making new friends.

I turned and started to pat Candy again, I told Ali, "I'd like to go and pat the pretty grey Arabian".

Ali replied,, "Well, good luck with that, he hasn't let anyone near him. But hey, why not give it a go. I'll come with you."

As we made our way to the front of the stables, we had to pass by the "mean girls". I couldn't help but notice their stink-eye and hushed giggles. I was definitely not feeling the warmest welcome, and honestly, it was pretty rude. I felt so uncomfortable.

However, as we walked by, the ringleader of the mean girls, Karin, decided to take a jab. She asked Ali, "Oh, what are you doing, Ali? Trying to pat that horse again for the millionth time? You know you're not the horse whisperer?" The girls all laughed and high-fived each other, revelling in their little joke.

Ali, never one to back down replied with a sarcastic tone, "Oh, Karin, you're just so funny." Then, she rolled her eyes and leaned in toward me, whispering, "Small minds do small things." I couldn't help but smirk at Ali's response, appreciating her confidence in the face of the mean girls' taunts.

As we got closer to the gate leading to the paddock with the mystery horse, I noticed that the mean girls were making their way to the front of the stable. It was pretty clear they intended to watch us and probably taunt us if we got rejected by the mysterious Arabian.

But you know what? Ali didn't let them get under her skin, so why should I? I decided to follow her lead and not give the mean girls the satisfaction of bothering us. Let's see how this meeting with the mystery horse goes!

I carefully opened the gate, and I could see the horse's head pop up from where he was munching on some grass, about halfway down his paddock. I stepped into the paddock and shut the gate behind me, while Ali climbed up onto the gate to watch.

I couldn't help but ask, "Does he have a name?"

Ali grinned and replied, "Nope, we have no idea where he came from, so I've been calling him 'Legs' for now. You know, because he's got these long legs and he's pretty like a supermodel." We both shared a laugh over the funny nick name she had given him. I can't imagine a horse like this would have such a simple name, but it seemed to fit him for now.

I kept my eyes on Legs as he started to walk toward me. Thoughts swirled in my head, including who could possibly own such a beautiful horse, and what his true name might be.

Suddenly, Ali let out a soft squeal and said, "Addison, I think he likes you! He's coming to you!"

Surprised, Ali asked, "Wait, what day did you say you arrived in town?"

"Last Sunday," I replied.

Ali's excitement was contagious, and she couldn't help but marvel at the coincidence. Little did we know, as you'll discover throughout this story, that there's no such thing as a coincidence, and everything will eventually tie together and make sense in the end.

I remembered what my mom had taught me from a young age about horses being able to read people's energy. It's like they could sense your intentions, and that's why some horses are drawn to certain people and repelled by others. If your intentions aren't genuine, horses can totally pick up on it. So, I stood still and held my hand out as Legs got closer. I wanted to make sure my energy was calm and friendly, hoping he'd sense that I was there with nothing but good intentions.

To my absolute surprise, Legs started to trot towards me, and as he reached me, he lowered his head, inviting me to pat him. I was completely awestruck, lost for words. His mane felt as soft as velvet under my touch, and I could sense his vibrant energy flowing through my fingers as I stroked his neck.

I whispered, "Hello there, Legs. My name is Addison."

Suddenly, Ali burst into laughter and yelled out to the mean girls, who were still watching and probably hoping for a laugh or a chance to tease us. "Looks like we're not horse whisperers, ladies, but Addison sure is! Did you see that, girls? He didn't just walk to her; he trotted!" She followed it up with a triumphant, "YEHAHHHH! Go Addison, go Legs!"

I couldn't help but smile as I looked up and saw the expressions of disappointment and embarrassment on the mean girls' faces. They stormed off like a bunch of rats in the night, clearly not expecting that outcome. Just then, my mom and one of the instructors came out to see me patting Legs. The instructor's name was Jill; she looked not only shocked but downright dumbfounded, as he usually chased off anyone who dared to enter his paddock.

My mom had a big smile on her face and said, "Looks like you've made some new friends," while watching me pat Legs and noticing Ali still perched on the gate.

Ali chimed in, "Hi Addison's mum! I'm Ali, and my horse Candy is the gorgeous Palomino in the stables. Isn't it awesome that Legs is letting Addison pat him?"

"Well, hello, Ali. Call me Kerri," my mom responded. "And yes, I had the pleasure of meeting your beautiful Candy during a stable tour with Jill earlier. I'm glad you and Addison have connected."

Jill added, "Well, since it's clear that you and this horse have a connection, you can work with him if you'd like. We'll wait to see if anyone comes to claim him. So far, no one around here has ever seen him before. You're the first person he's let near him, so I guess he's laying claim to you. Just remember, we know nothing about him or if he's broken in, so be careful when working with him and stay safe."

Ali couldn't help but bring up the coincidence, saying, "Jill, we worked out that Addison and Legs arrived in town on the same day. How funny is that?"

Jill nodded in agreement and replied, "Maybe it's just fate that you two are meant to be together."

While my mom and Jill were having a chat, Ali hopped down from the gate and joined me by Legs. She wondered aloud if he'd let her pat him now that I was there. Ali cautiously extended her hand and began to pat him gently. To our amazement, Legs didn't flinch or back away.

Ali couldn't contain her excitement, exclaiming, "Wow, he feels so soft, like no other horse I've ever patted!"

I couldn't help but nod in agreement with Ali's words. "I thought the same, Ali. As weird as this sounds, Legs doesn't feel like a normal horse. There's something special about him, something magical."

Ali nodded in response; her eyes still locked on Legs. "I think you're right, Addy."

She suddenly glanced at her watch, and a look of panic crossed her face. "Oh wow, I'm running late. I need to go help my dad unload the fish from his boat at the pier. It's my part-time job to help pay for my horse obsession."

I chuckled and replied, "OMG, that's what my dad and bro say about my mom and me, that we're just horse obsessed."

We both shared a laugh in agreement, bonding over our shared passion. Ali then made an unexpected offer. "Hey, do you want to come with me to the pier? You can see where I live, and I can tell you about some of the town legends on the way."

Excitement bubbled up inside me as I responded, "Yes, I would love to. Let me go ask my mom."

We both patted Legs goodbye for now and began walking towards the gate. To our surprise, Legs decided to follow us, almost like a loyal dog, stopping when we did and walking when we moved forward. Ali grinned and said, "Well, you've made three friends today: me, Candy, and Legs. You're off to a good start for the new girl in town."

CHAPTER TWO
THE TOWN TALES

My mom agreed to let me go with Ali and reminded me, "Be home before dark." I couldn't help but smile; it was a rule my mother had grown up with as well. Home before dark and always let her or dad know where I was going. It seemed fair enough, and I gave her a quick nod of agreement before heading off with Ali, excited to see where Ali lived and hear about the town's tales and legends.

Ali asked if I needed to assist my mom before leaving because she used a wheelchair. I told Ali how incredibly independent my mom was, needing minimal help. My mom could drive and manage her wheelchair herself since it could come apart and fit next to her in the passenger seat. Ali was intrigued by my mom's self-reliance and apologised for asking about it, explaining that she had never met someone who used a wheelchair before. I totally understood and appreciated her curiosity. I was used to such questions, but I realised it was a new experience for her.

Ali and I wrapped up packing her stuff at the stable, said goodbye to Candy and then Legs, and began our walk down the driveway toward the pier. Curiosity got the better of me, and I couldn't help but ask, "How long have you lived here?"

Ali smiled and replied, "I was born here, like my father and his father, and the one before that. Our family is one of the original families that settled when Port Cooper was founded a million and one years ago. Well, maybe not that long ago, but it sure feels like it when you've lived in the same town all your life."

We both shared a giggle at the thought, and I couldn't help but feel a sense of history and connection to this place as I walked alongside her.

Excitement bubbled up in me, and I asked, "Tell me about some of the town's tales and legends. I love spooky, creepy stuff and mysteries."

Ali's laughter continued as she added, "My dad is the town's storyteller. Sometimes, you're not sure what's true or not because his tales are so far-fetched, but he swears blue they're all real. He's been telling me for years about how he sees mermaids in the bay."

My eyes widened with fascination. "Mermaids? Seriously?"

Ali nodded with a mischievous grin. "Oh yeah, and that's just the tip of the iceberg. We've got haunted lighthouses, buried pirate treasures, and a mysterious ghost ship with ghost pirates that are said to appear coming out of the ocean on moonless nights. The legends here are like a mix of adventure and spookiness, and they've been passed down through generations."

My excitement grew as we walked towards the pier, and I couldn't help but share my own titbit of information. "WOW, have you seen the walls at The Haunted Lilly? It's like a storybook for all the things you just told me. Pirate ships, mermaids, and other weird stuff. Like the big wooden mermaid out front."

Ali's eyes lit up. "Oh, yes, The Haunted Lilly. That place is a treasure trove of weird and spooky stories. And that wooden mermaid? It's got a legend of its own. They say it's a talisman that wards off sea curses and brings good fortune to the town."

As we continued chatting about the town's mysteries and legends, I couldn't help but feel like I was diving headfirst into a thrilling adventure, and I was loving every moment of it. Just then, we arrived at the pier and walked towards her dad's boat. I looked around at the different boats tied to the pier.

Having been born and raised in the Arizona desert, being so close to the ocean now felt like an entirely different world. The scent of the saltwater and the taste of the sea breeze were all new sensations for me. Yet, strangely, they brought me an odd feeling of comfort and peace. It was as if I had found a place where I truly belonged. It felt like home.

Ali's tap on my arm snapped me out of my daydream, and I quickly refocused on the present. "There's my dad and his boat. Come and meet him," she said, with excitement. Without wasting a moment, she started running toward the boat, squealing with joy as she yelled, "Hi Dad!"

I followed Ali with a grin, eager to meet her dad and immerse myself further in this new and exciting coastal world that was quickly becoming my home.

Ali introduced me to her dad with a warm smile, "Dad, this is my new friend Addison. Her family just moved here a week ago from America, and they took over The Haunted Lilly pub and live there now. I met Addison and her mum at the stables this afternoon."

Ali's dad, Troy, extended his hand with a friendly grin, saying, "Hi Addison! Lovely to meet you. Call me Troy. Is your mom Kerri?"

I replied, "Yes, that's my mom. Do you know her?"

Troy smiled and said, "Yes, we went to school together. I've known your mom for a very long time. I heard she was back in town when she inherited the Haunted Lilly. I'll have to stop by and say hello".

As I shook his hand, I continued, "Nice to meet you too. I'm sure you have some fun stories about my mom and I'm sure she would love to see you and catch up."

"Ali's been showing me around and telling me all about the town's legends. It's been amazing."

Troy laughed heartily and agreed, "Yes, one thing this town never lacks are stories and legends."

Ali, eager to share her dad's tale, chimed in, "Tell Addy about the mermaids you see when out at sea, Dad."

My eyes widened with curiosity, and I leaned in, eager to hear Troy spill the tea about these mysterious mermaids.

Troy began to share his captivating tale, "Oh yes, it's a story that's been told for hundreds of years about mermaids, or sirens as some call them. They're said to call out to sailors and fishermen to lure them to their death. I've seen many of them come up close to the boat, only to dart away when we make eye contact.

It used to freak me out when I was a young boy, until my dad told me it's a rite of passage for all true fishermen to see mermaids. You're not a sailor or fisherman until you do."

I listened with rapt attention, completely fascinated by the idea of mermaids and the stories that had been passed down through generations in this town. It was like stepping into a world where every day held the promise of adventure and mystery.

As Troy mentioned the daylight fading and the need to get the fish into the shop, I quickly offered to help. "I'd love to help you and Ali, so we can get it done quicker," I said, eager to be part of this new experience. "But I'll have to head home before dark, as I promised my mom."

Ali and her dad both thanked me for the offer, and we set to work together, swiftly unloading the fish from the boat. It felt like a bonding experience, and I was excited to be a part of Ali's world and the vibrant community of Port Cooper.

Ali shared with me on our walk to the pier that her mom passed away when she was just a baby, so it's been her dad and her grandma, Alice, who raised her. Not surprisingly, they own the local fish shop right on the pier, and lived upstairs. Her dad, being one of the fishermen here, adds to this crazy rich history of the town. It was clear that for families like Ali's, Port Cooper wasn't just a spot on the map; it was part of their very identity, a place that had been home to generations of their family. It was amazing to see how the town's history was intricately woven into their own family story.

As we finished unloading the last load of fish from the boat and walking towards the shop, we noticed a boat pulling up close to the front of the pier. We couldn't help but slow down to take a look at the damaged boat—it was hard to miss, with a massive gaping hole on the side of it. The fisherman who had just stepped off the boat approached Troy. Ali and I couldn't help but stop to eavesdrop on their conversation, our curiosity at an all-time high.

The fisherman's words sent a shiver down my spine. "Hey, Troy, our boats are being attacked again," he said, and I was shocked to hear the word "again" like it wasn't something new around here. Troy's surprise mirrored my own, and he replied, "Well, it's been a while since any of us had a boat attacked, though."

The fisherman explained, "It started last Sunday when Jimmy's boat was attacked out at sea. He was lucky to get back in without any major damage. But clearly, I wasn't as lucky. I really thought I was going down this time Troy. It's getting worse. I'm quitting. I'm moving to the city."

Ali's words made my heart race as she connected the dots. "Last Sunday, that's when you arrived, and that's when Legs arrived."

The timing of these events was uncanny, and it left me with a sense that there was something much more mysterious and perhaps even dangerous lurking beneath the surface of this charming coastal town.

The mystery surrounding the boat attacks had my curiosity in overdrive, and I turned to Ali with questions swirling in my mind. "What could be attacking the boats? Is it mermaids or some kind of sea monster?"

Ali's words sent chills down my spine, "No, not mermaids, but some type of sea creature, something huge. It can snap boats in half like a twig and drag them down to the bottom of the ocean. No one has survived a major attack to tell anyone what it is. You're lucky if you get back with only a hole in your boat. But it's been like 20 years since that all happened. I remember my dad and grandfather talking about the boat attacks from the '90s."

The fact that these attacks had occurred a while ago and were now resurfacing added an extra layer of mystery to the situation. I couldn't help but wonder what could have triggered these events to start happening again.

31

The idea of a massive, unknown sea creature prowling the waters around Port Copper filled me with both fear and fascination. It was like something out of a thrilling adventure story, but this was real life, and the danger was real.

Lost in thought, I suddenly realised that the sun had disappeared, and it was now dark. Panic set in as I remembered my promise to my parents about returning home before dark. I quickly excused myself, saying, "I need to get home; I'm already late."

Before I left, Troy, Ali's dad, insisted, "Here, Addison, please take this home to your parents for dinner. And I look forward to catching up with your mom and meeting your dad soon." He handed me two big fish wrapped in paper. I thanked him warmly for the generous gesture and started to make my way home, determined to get there as quickly as possible and avoid any further trouble.

Ali yelled out, "Meet me tomorrow at the stables so we can ride Candy on the beach and hang out."

Ali's invitation filled me with excitement, and I eagerly accepted, shouting back, "YES! Thank you and see you tomorrow if I'm not grounded."

As I hurried home through the darkening streets of Port Cooper, the sound of loud splashing beneath the pier caught my attention. An eerie feeling washed over me, and I couldn't resist investigating. I cautiously approached the edge of the pier, gripping the railing tightly as I peered over, my heart pounding.

What I saw sent a chill down my spine—something large was moving beneath the water, causing the splashing noises. I couldn't make out what it was due to the darkness, but it seriously creeped me out, and without thinking twice, I turned and sprinted in the direction of The Haunted Lilly as fast as my legs could carry me. The unknown and the eerie atmosphere of Port Cooper were becoming all too real.

The unknown and the image of the massive hole in the damaged boat haunted my thoughts. What could possibly cause such destruction? The mysteries of Port Cooper seemed to grow deeper by the minute. My curiosity got the best of me, and I decided I would examine the walls of The Haunted Lilly pub for any hints or clues. I hoped the paintings on those walls might reveal some secrets, like cave paintings from indigenous people, telling stories of past years. Maybe some answers to my many questions.

As I was about to enter The Haunted Lilly, I couldn't resist stopping to take a closer look at the huge wooden mermaid. Despite the fading and chipping paint from age, she had an enchanting yet slightly unnerving vibe about her. I couldn't help but wonder who had made this mermaid and how much truth there was in the mermaid stories that had been passed down through generations.

The idea that Ali's dad, Troy, had actually seen these mermaids added a layer of mystery. Was he hamming it up or telling the truth? There was a saying that all folktales started from some kernel of truth, and that notion danced around in my mind as I gazed at the wooden figure. It was as if the mermaid held the key to unlocking the secrets of Port Cooper.

The sudden opening of the front door startled me while I was lost in thought, causing me to jump and let out a scream. It was my mom, and her stern voice immediately made me feel guilty. "Well, nice of you to show up, Addison. You know the rules, and it's dark and has been for a while."

I quickly apologised and entered the pub, explaining how I had lost track of time. I shared the story of helping Ali and her dad with unloading the fish from the boat and how one fisherman had a massive hole in his boat. My mom listened with a mix of concern and understanding, and as I spoke, I couldn't help but feel a sense of relief to be back home, even if it meant facing some consequences for breaking curfew.

My dad entered the room and joined the conversation. He asked why I was late, and I eagerly launched into the story of my eventful day. I recounted my visit to the riding school, my encounter with Ali, and the mystery horse named Legs. I told them about our trip to the pier, where I had the chance to meet Ali's dad, Troy, and hear the mysterious tales of the sea monster attacks on boats. And, of course, I mentioned how Troy went to school with my mom. It was a day full of exciting discoveries.

In the midst of my storytelling, I suddenly remembered that I was still holding the paper-wrapped fish. "Oh, here," I said, handing them the package. "Troy, Ali's dad, gave these to us for dinner." My parents looked surprised but grateful for the unexpected gift, and we continued talking about the day's adventures and the mysteries of Port Cooper.

I shared all the details with my parents, emphasising Troy's claims about the mermaids and how he had seen them with his own eyes. Then, I told them about my plan to examine the walls of The Haunted Lilly, hoping that the old artwork might reveal a story about the mermaids and pirates. The events of the day had left me with so many questions.

My brother, Ethan, walked into the room, and I couldn't wait to spill the beans about my epic day. And then, I shared my genius plan to investigate The Haunted Lilly's walls for any clues. You won't believe it, but Ethan, who's a total adventure enthusiast like me, got super pumped and said, "Let's do it!" So, off we went, scouring every nook and cranny of the bar, checking out all those ancient paintings and pictures. Seriously, it was like a treasure trove of quirky stuff that's been collected over the years.

My parents actually got super excited and offered to help us with our search at The Haunted Lilly. It was a family adventure in the making. With their assistance, we hoped to uncover the secrets hidden within the artwork on the pub's walls.

I slowly walked through The Haunted Lilly, my eyes fixed firmly on the walls, where an epic story seemed to unfold right there in the paintings and pictures. There were mermaids, fierce pirates, sunken ships resting at the ocean's floor, missing treasures, and get this… There were these giant tentacles wrapping around ships! But it didn't stop there. I also saw these mermaids doing a total shape-shifting thing, going from sea creatures to humans right on the beach. And there were seahorses and regular horses, like, merging with the ocean. It was a wild mix of fantasy and reality, and I couldn't shake the feeling that these walls were trying to tell some epic tale about Port Cooper. I couldn't help but feel like there was a whole world of secrets and legends just waiting to be uncovered on these walls.

So, there I was, all pumped about uncovering the secrets hidden in those wall paintings. However, my dad and brother got totally side-tracked. They started blabbering about knocking down walls and creating a stage for bands. I mean, seriously? We were in the middle of a mystery hunt here! I tried to remind them that we were on the hunt for clues about the town's folk tales, but they were already deep into their building plans. My mom, with a dramatic eyeroll, said, "Let them be. We can figure it out together after dinner. Let's get that fish cooked up."

And just like that, my epic investigation was put on hold for dinner. While I helped mom with dinner, I couldn't help but bring up my thoughts about the big mermaid statue at the front entrance of The Haunted Lilly. It was in pretty rough shape, with paint peeling off, and honestly, she looked like she needed a makeover. I told mom that this grand old lady of a statue deserved some serious help and sprucing up.

I was so stoked when mom said she'd help fix up the mermaid statue, the one she called "Lilly." She even talked about getting some sandpaper and paint to make her all shiny and pretty again. I couldn't help but get curious about the story behind that mermaid and how it's linked to The Haunted Lilly pub, especially given her connection to the pub. I was kinda beat, though, and didn't have the energy to bug her with a million questions right then. But one thing was certain: I couldn't wait for our project to bring our tired old mermaid, Lilly, back to life.

After we discussed the mermaid makeover, I suddenly remembered my plans with Ali to take Candy to the beach tomorrow. So, I mustered up the courage and asked my mom if it would be okay to go later, after helping out around The Haunted Lilly in the morning. I knew there was a lot of cleaning up to do, and they needed my help. But at the same time, I was kind of testing the waters to see if I was going to get grounded for not getting home on time tonight.

To my surprise, my mom was actually happy for me to have made a friend and encouraged me to go off and have some horse fun with Ali. It was like getting a green light for a new adventure, and I couldn't have been more excited. But she assured me if I was not home before dark this time I would be grounded. I agreed that was fair and promised I'd be home in time.

So, we all sat down for dinner in the massive dining room of the pub, and seriously, it looked like it had seen better days. It was screaming for a makeover too, but honestly, you could totally see how this place could be epic and become a massive tourist hotspot once it was all fixed up.

My dad and brother were deep into discussing the rooms they worked on upstairs today, and they were super enthusiastic about their plans for the place. They were excited about getting this stage set up for bands and fixing the bedrooms upstairs to welcome overnight guests. They even managed to get the old lift working, so now mom could access the top levels without my dad having to carry her up every time she needed to get there.

"We're officially wheelchair accessible now," Mom said with a big grin.

I was genuinely happy mom was totally independent again. I knew how much she hated relying on dad carrying her up and down the stairs. I was also pumped about dad and my brother's stage idea. It sounded awesome, and it perfectly blended their love for renovations and music. The Haunted Lilly had its own epic story and vibe, and it deserved to be shared with the world. It could totally become the tourist attraction it used to be before it fell into disrepair. I couldn't help but daydream about all the incredible things this place could turn into!

After dinner, I was exhausted and all I just wanted was to shower and get some rest. I said good night to my folks and my brother and headed upstairs to my room. As I slowly climbed the steps, I couldn't help but notice how gross the carpet was. But then, something caught my eye; a painting on the wall halfway up the stairs.

I legit stopped dead in my tracks. In that painting, there was a white horse, running free on the beach, and it seriously looked just like Legs. But here's the wild part: in the background, there was a pirate ship and some freakin' mermaids, just chillin' and watching the horse, right in between the boat and the land.

I mean, it was the quirkiest and oddest painting ever, and I had to snap a pic of it with my cell phone. I was like, "Ali has to see this tomorrow!" 'Cause seriously, who would believe this without seeing it? It was just that totally wild and a little creepy at the same time.

As I entered my new room, I was reminded it was also in desperate need of a makeover to reflect my personality. Its outdated design felt like a blast from the past, and nothing about it screamed "cool teenager." My parents had given me the green light to redecorate it. However, with our belongings still on their way from the U.S by boat, that could be weeks away, even months. There wasn't much I could do about it just yet. Nonetheless, I had big plans for it once our stuff arrived. I envisioned stripping off the old wallpaper and painting the walls in bright, cheerful fun colours—maybe even pink, my all-time favourite colour. Yes, I know it's a bit girly but I love how it makes me feel happy and joyful. I want my room to be a vibrant and happy space that truly feels like mine. I couldn't wait to hang up photos of my horses from back in the U.S. and display the ribbons I had won during my days as a competitive rider. My room was going to be a reflection of my passion for horses and all things pink, showing my own unique style. I had it all planned out in my head and now it was just a waiting game until I could put my vision into action.

As I grabbed my towel to go have a shower, I thought about how the whole day was like a wild rollercoaster ride, and honestly, since we landed in Port Cooper, it had been one bizarre and eerie thing after another. But here was the crazy part: even though I had been a bit freaked out at times, I somewhat felt strangely comfortable here. I have always loved an adventure and I'm totally into thriller and suspense movies. So, this appeared as though I was living in my own adventure movie. I couldn't shake the feeling that something significant was on the horizon, but I wasn't sure what that "something" was.

Yet, I found myself drawn to the thrill of the unknown and the anticipation of a grand adventure.

After my wonderful, long hot shower and all that thinking and trying to piece things together, I was totally tossing and turning in bed all night. It was like my mind was on overdrive, trying to figure out what those paintings meant and how all these crazy things in Port Cooper were connected. What was the message? There was always a message right? But eventually, I just passed out, because seriously, sometimes you've gotta let your brain take a break and hope that maybe, just maybe, some answers will come in your dreams.

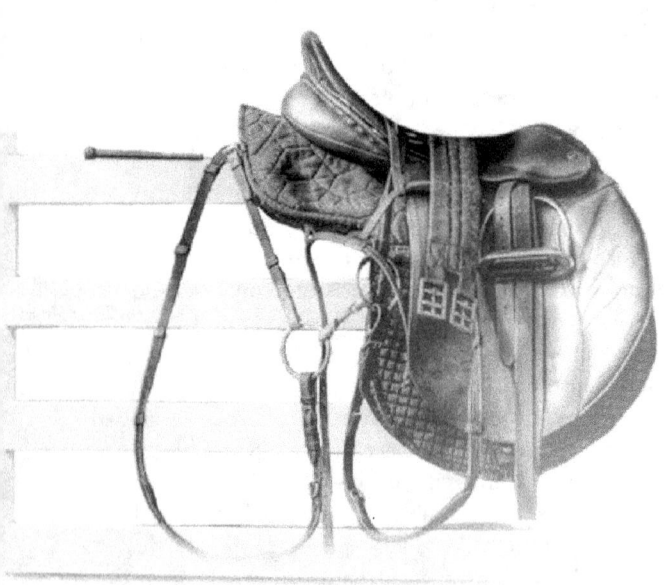

CHAPTER THREE
MISSING LEGS

I woke up totally pumped for another day of adventure in this town, wondering what surprises today would bring. But before I could dive into the day, I pitched in with my parents and my brother to help clean up and get things done around The Haunted Lilly. We were lugging around old carpets and broken timber, tossing them into that huge skip bin outside. Man, it was filling up fast, and I could tell it was gonna be a common sight as the pub got renovated.

So today was gonna get kinda of wild around here. My dad and brother had this big master plan to demolish some walls and turn our cramped rooms into, you know, useful spaces. I guess it was a good idea, my bedroom wasn't that big, and I needed more space being a growing teenager.

But honestly, I was just relieved that I'd be hanging out with Ali and Candy for the rest of the day. I mean, seriously, who wants to stick around for all that crazy noise, with hammers banging and stuff crashing down? Besides, it was boring—certainly not with this girl, no way!

I grabbed my beach gear and made a beeline for the stables before anyone could rope me into doing more chores. As I hightailed it towards the riding stables—which were only a quick 10-minute walk from The Haunted Lilly—my mind was on overdrive, replaying all the wild stuff that went down yesterday.

I couldn't wait to be with Legs and get back to having a blast on the beach with Ali and Candy. But what had me totally stoked was the thought of digging even deeper into the epic stories this town's known for.

And, oh my gosh, the mermaids! I've been low-key obsessed with mermaids since I was a little kid, but now that there was even a tiny chance, they could be real. That's like next-level crazy! I was practically bursting with excitement to learn more about all these wild stories and legends Port Cooper had to offer.

As I started to walk down the driveway at the riding school, I was super excited to see Legs again. However, when I started looking around, I couldn't spot him anywhere. I even got closer to the fence, scanning both sides, but there was still no sign of him.

I couldn't believe my eyes when I couldn't find Legs anywhere in the paddock. Panic was starting to set in. Where the heck could he be? I even went inside his paddock for a closer look, and still, no sign of Legs. My heart was sinking fast, and I was starting to think the worst—maybe his owner came to claim him.

I rushed back to the gate, closed it, and headed towards the stables in a hurry. That's when I spotted Karin, standing there with that smug look on her face. I was totally expecting some snarky remark from her, but she didn't say a word and simply looked satisfied that I couldn't find Legs.

I ignored her and walked straight past and went into the stable office. I needed answers, and I needed them now. I knocked on the door as I entered in a rush, and Jill greeted me warmly with a, "Hello, Addison."

I wasted no time and asked her, "What happened to Legs? Did someone come and claim him?"

Jill looked just as puzzled as I felt as we exchanged baffled glances. She shrugged and said, "Yeah, seriously! It's a total mystery. We came out this morning to feed him, and poof, he's gone. The gate was shut tight, and it's like he vanished into thin air."

Gone? Who in the world could have taken him? I was utterly confused.

Just then, Ali showed up at the office door, wanting to know what all the fuss was about. I quickly filled her in on the Legs' situation and how he'd gone missing, and the gate being shut. It was clear that Legs hadn't simply run off on his own.

Ali turned to Karin, who happened to be conveniently close to the office door, probably trying to listen in on our conversation. She shot straight at Karin, asking, "So, what's your story in all of this, Karin?"

Tension hung in the air, and I braced myself for some kind of snarky comeback from Karin. But instead, she just chuckled and played it cool, saying, "Oh, come on, relax. I didn't do anything to your precious Legs." Jill, sensing the rising tension, acted like a peacemaker. She stepped in and urged us all to cool our jets, explaining that Legs had vanished just as mysteriously as he'd shown up. She didn't have any explanations, so we had to take a deep breath and cross our fingers that he might reappear.

Boy, it was a tough one to digest. The whole Legs mystery was like a puzzle with missing pieces, and it left us all scratching our heads and feeling pretty darn baffled and frustrated.

Ali's idea of hitting the beach with Candy to relax and enjoy the day sounded like a much-needed distraction from the whole Legs mystery. So, we headed over to Candy's stable to get ready.

While we were getting Candy all set for our beach adventure, I couldn't help but voice my thoughts to Ali about Legs. "Isn't it just super weird that he would bounce like that? I mean, if his owner was around, you'd expect them to at least show up and prove they were the real deal, right? What do you think might've gone down?" The whole situation was like this big, puzzling riddle, and I was dying to know what Ali made of it.

Ali's response mirrored my own feelings of confusion about the whole situation. "I honestly have no idea," she said. "As mean as Karin is, I doubt she did anything to hurt him. She's just mean with her words. It's all just so strange, isn't it?"

The mystery of Legs weighed on our minds, and it was becoming increasingly clear that there was more to the story than met the eye. Still, we decided to set it aside for the moment and focus on the beach day ahead with Candy. Dwelling on the missing horse wouldn't do us any good, and we were determined to make the most of our time in the sun and sand.

Ali suddenly pulled off her backpack which stirred my curiosity, and I couldn't help but wonder what she had up her sleeve. With an excited glint in her eye, she started digging around inside and then exclaimed, "I've got something seriously cool to show you."

Just like that, she unveiled this absolutely incredible, massive seashell. It was one of those shells you usually only see in movies. You know, the kind that you can blow into to produce this hauntingly beautiful, echoing sound. But this shell was on a whole different level. It had this mesmerising pearlescent sheen that was just breath-taking.

As Ali handed me the shell, and I cradled it in my hands, entranced by its sheer beauty, she casually dropped a bombshell of her own. This wasn't just your run-of-the-mill seashell; it was said to have the power to summon mermaids. My eyes practically popped out of my head in shock, and I couldn't help but blurt out, "No way, seriously?"

Ali went on to unravel the shell's family history. She told me that her dad believed it was a truly magical shell with the power to summon mermaids. It had been passed down from generation to generation in their family, starting from her granddad to her dad. I was captivated by the tale and couldn't resist asking the million-dollar question, "Did it ever actually work?"

Ali just chuckled and replied, "Well, my dad gave it a shot once, and nada, zip, zero mermaids. But it's a cool story, and the shell's pretty awesome, so he keeps it in the fish and chip shop as a fun prop. Whenever tourists ask about it, he tells them it's a mermaid cell phone."

We both had a good laugh at the quirky story, finding it both fascinating and hilariously entertaining.

Ali's plan to bring the enchanting mermaid-summoning seashell to the beach sounded like an absolute blast, especially given all the mysterious happenings in town lately. The afternoon was shaping up to be an exciting one, filled with beachside adventures alongside Ali, Candy, and the prospect of discovering more intriguing folktales.

Once we finished getting Candy ready, with a good brush down, picking out her hooves, and putting on a bridle, Ali told me that Candy loved the beach. She mentioned that we'd be "double dinking" on Candy to get to the beach. I must've had a puzzled look on my face when I asked, "What does 'double dink' mean?" Ali burst into giggles and explained that it's Australian slang for riding together on one horse. We both had a good laugh about the language differences, and I was definitely looking forward to our ride to the beach.

Ali grabbed her backpack, the one holding the mystical mermaid seashell, along with some drinks and snacks. I suddenly felt a twinge of guilt for not bringing some snacks and drinks myself. So, I suggested, "Hey, maybe we could swing by The Haunted Lilly, and I can grab some stuff, too."

Ali, being as awesome as ever, assured me, "Nah, it's all good. I've got enough for both of us, and some carrots for Candy, too." Her kindness put a smile on my face, and I couldn't wait to start on our beach adventure with such a great friend and her beautiful horse, Candy.

As I prepared to hop onto Candy, Ali's keen eyes spotted the birthmark on my inner right arm. She seemed genuinely impressed and complimented, "Hey, that's a really cool birthmark. It's shaped like a perfect heart."

I chuckled and replied, "Yeah, it's pretty neat. Some folks have even asked if it's a tattoo because it's so perfectly shaped, but nope, I'm only 14, so definitely not a tattoo." We both shared a good laugh, and it was a nice, light-hearted moment before we embarked on our beach adventure.

I climbed onto the back of Candy, with Ali riding in front, and together we set off down the driveway, "double dinking" our way towards the beach. Australian slang never failed to crack me up; it felt like this special language that only Australians truly got. But after being Down Under for about two weeks now, I was starting to catch on and find my way around it.

My dad and my brother are totally into using Aussie slang any chance they get. Dad's all about, "I need a cold one" for a cold beer, and he's always dropping "Avro" short for afternoon. My brother, on the other hand, is all about "ankle biter" for a kid, and he can't resist saying, "Barbie" when it's barbecue time. Seriously, it's like they pick topics just to throw in some slang they just learnt, but it's actually pretty hilarious to listen to.

I snapped out of my Aussie slang daydream and enjoyed being back on a horse. It felt absolutely amazing. Even though it had only been a couple of weeks since I'd last ridden, it felt like months. Riding had a soothing effect on my soul, bringing me peace and distraction from worrying about Legs and all the mysteries in Port Cooper.

I do have a habit of overthinking things, but I just can't help it. This afternoon was the perfect way to spend time with my new friends, Ali and Candy.

As we rode toward the beach, Ali spilled the beans about this incredible riding spot she adored. It was peaceful and away from the touristy craziness in town. I couldn't help but notice that Port Cooper seemed to be a magnet for tourists, so I asked Ali what made this place so darn special that it drew in all these visitors, given that Australia had plenty of towns with gorgeous beaches.

Ali explained that the town's popularity among tourists was linked to a few intriguing folktales that attracted treasure and ghost hunters. According to the stories, many years ago, pirates had stopped in Port Cooper to rest, resupply, and indulge in heavy drinking, as pirates often do. They got so drunk that one of them ran off with their treasure. When the other pirates caught him later that night, the gold was gone, and they assumed he had buried it. Since then, pirates had been coming to the town in search of that lost treasure. The treasure was said to have also had a special amulet with magical abilities.

This got me really curious, and I asked Ali, "Magical abilities, like what?"

Ali replied, "Well, the rumour is that it allowed the user to be immortal." My eyes widened in amazement, and I couldn't wait to hear more about these intriguing legends.

Ali had my full attention as she continued with her story. She hesitated for a moment and then said, "Well, it's also said that the ghosts of these pirates come looking for the treasure and the amulet, and they've been seen here in Port Cooper."

My curiosity was at an all-time high now as I leaned in closer, asking, "Why shouldn't you tell me this part?"

Ali replied, "It's got to do with where you're living, at The Haunted Lilly."

My eyes widened, and I felt a chill run down my spine. I needed to know more, so I urged Ali to continue. She hesitated again, looking a bit unsure, but I nodded and said, "Please, tell me."

Ali then shared a chilling tale about The Haunted Lilly. Apparently, the pub used to offer overnight stays up until only a few years ago before my mom's aunt closed it down. The rooms were always fully booked, with guests hoping to catch a glimpse of ghosts. Some people were so terrified that they left in the middle of the night. That's how the pub got its name, "The Haunted Lilly." The wooden mermaid outside the entrance is named Lilly after a fisherman from over a hundred years ago claimed he had met a mermaid named Lilly. It was originally called "The Local Lilly," but when ghost sightings became more frequent, the owners at the time cashed in on the public's interest and changed it to "The Haunted Lilly."

I was totally captivated by Ali's storytelling. "Wow, you know so much!" I exclaimed.

Ali let out a laugh and replied, "Well, I've grown up in this town with my dad always spinning these incredible tales."

Right on cue, we arrived at that secluded beach spot Ali had raved about, and it was even more incredible than I'd imagined. It was like stumbling upon a hidden treasure chest, the perfect haven for us to soak up the sun without being swarmed by other beach lovers.

CHAPTER FOUR
THE MERMAID CELL PHONE

Without wasting a second, we got to work, setting up our mini beach oasis. Towels spread out, beach umbrella set up, snacks within arm's reach, and the mermaid-seashell-treasure in a safe spot, we were all set for a day of beachside adventures and fun. We stripped down to our swimsuits, all set for a day of beachy fun, ready to ride Candy and dive into the water. The sun was beaming down, and the ocean was sparkling and oh-so-inviting with its shimmering waves.

Ali handed me the sunscreen, stressing the importance of shielding ourselves from the blazing Australian sun. We both shared a chuckle, and I reminded her that I came from the scorching heat of Arizona, so I knew the drill. We had a good laugh about that one.

I was so pumped to feel the salty waves against my skin and in my hair as we frolicked and galloped along the beach.

We spent what felt like a gazillion hours riding around in the water, out of the water, and cantering along the shoreline. We were double dinking and going solo, just having an absolute blast. I swear, I had this giant grin plastered on my face from ear to ear, and I couldn't stop laughing. Chilling with Ali and riding Candy was beyond amazing. They were like the ultimate team, and I was so grateful we became friends.

When I was with them, all those homesick feelings just melted away. It was genuinely the best day ever!

We took a break and sat down to enjoy the lunch that Ali had packed for us along with some ice-cold drinks. Ali reached into her backpack and retrieved the little ice chest containing our drinks. She also took out the large mermaid shell she had shown me earlier at the stables and handed it to me. As she fed some carrots to Candy, Ali encouraged me to give the shell a try and see what happens. I couldn't help but laugh as I accepted the shell from her.

I gave it my best shot, trying to blow into the shell, but I was failing miserably, and I couldn't stop laughing at how silly I looked while trying. Ali couldn't help but laugh along with me. Amidst our giggles, she leaned in and said, "Nah, you're doing it all wrong. Watch this." She took the shell, with one hand on either end, and then she gave it a good blow.

And oh boy, did it work! The shell produced this enchanting, humming call sound that was honestly pretty indescribable but cool. We both just sat there, mesmerised by the magical sound, grinning like crazy.

After Ali showed me how to use the shell, she handed it back and encouraged, "Okay, now it's your turn." I copied her technique and blew hard into the shell. But to our surprise, it produced a completely different sound than when Ali did it. It was way louder and kind of ear-piercing, like it was calling out to something or maybe even giving a warning.

Ali's eyes widened in shock, and she asked, "Wow, what was that?"

I stopped and replied, "I don't know, why is it so different from when you did it?"

Ali shook her head and said, "I have no idea, but do it again."

I raised the shell to my lips and blew into it again, and both Ali and I kept our eyes fixed on the sea. Suddenly we saw something coming out of the water, gradually making its way toward the shore. My excitement was through the roof, and I couldn't help but shout, "OMG, what is that?!"

Ali, just as thrilled as I was, urged me to do it once more. So, I took a deep breath and blew into the shell again.

Okay, let me stop here for a minute to explain. It was at this very moment that my life changed forever. This is just a part of the secret I'm about to reveal. It was this exact moment I discovered that magic is real, and magical beings exist. Maybe not all, but this one was about to appear before me as I continued to blow into the mermaid shell.

48

We both stared in utter shock at what was emerging from the ocean – it was LEGS!!! Yes, you read that right, as in Legs, the horse from the stable that had gone missing. He had just morphed from the ocean into a horse right in front of our eyes. I turned to Ali, completely baffled, and said, "OMG, are you seeing this? Am I dreaming?" Ali, with her jaw dropped and a frozen expression, seemed just as stunned as me. I had to snap her out of it, shouting,
"ALI, HELLO!"

She finally came to her senses and burst into laughter. "WHAT THE HELL just happened?" She laughed. I joined in her laughter, a mix of fear and nerves adding to the hysteria.

As Legs walked right up to us, completely soaked from emerging from the ocean, Ali stopped laughing just long enough to say, "You called him from the shell. He came to you."

I was still in shock as I began to pat him.

Out of nowhere, Ali unleashed this mega scream, and she was totally pointing at something on Legs' head.

"OMG, ADDISON, CHECK THIS OUT!!!"

Her scream was piercing, startling me. I quickly scrambled to the front of Legs to see what in the world she was losing it over. And there it was—a perfectly shaped heart, clearly marked on his wet forehead. I mean, it was so clear, he was all soaked from coming out of the ocean. I stared at my arm and then back at Legs, and they totally matched. I was totally freaking out, yelling, "WHAT IS EVEN HAPPENING?!"

I glanced over at Ali, and we both started to completely lose it and started laughing like a couple of maniacs.

After we finally got a grip on ourselves and stopped laughing like loons, Ali dropped the big question, "So what do we even do now?"

I was still in shock, but I managed to pull myself together and said, "Dude, there's no way we can spill the beans on this. I mean, seriously, no one would believe us, and we'd probably end up in some loony bin or something."

We were totally on the same page about this, and we both knew it had to be our top-secret, just between us. No way could we spill the beans, not even to our folks, at least, not for now. So, we locked it in with a pinkie promise.

Ali made a totally solid point that blew my mind. She pointed out how there was clearly some type of crazy connection between me and Legs. He not only let me touch him at the stables, but he also showed up for me when I blew that shell, and we even had these matching heart markings on our bodies. It was seriously one weird and wacky mystery. I have to admit, as crazy as it was, it was also super cool and awesome. I mean, I had this mystical ocean horse that, for some reason, seemed to want only me.

At that moment, Legs knelt down on his front legs, inviting me to get on his back. Ali couldn't believe it, exclaiming, "WOW, get on him?" Despite some hesitation, I decided to go for it. With our inexplicable connection and the fact that Legs had just morphed from a seahorse into a horse in front of me, what could go wrong at this point?

I straight-up jumped onto Legs, gripping his mane as he stood there calmly. I gave Ali a look that said, "Yeah, I'm doing this."

Ali, now back on Candy, was like, "How 'bout we just ride along the shore?" And I swear, I was practically bursting with excitement. Riding Legs was an extraordinary adventure. We both laughed our heads off as we kicked off into a canter along the shoreline. The water was splashing all over us as the horses' legs splashed through the small shore waves, shooting sprays of seawater up into the air.

I mean, seriously, there I was, riding Legs, no saddle or bridle, just straight-up bareback. I started to relax and soak in this crazy and incredible moment. Like, who in their right mind could say they've ridden a magical ocean seahorse?

I started to relax and truly savour this moment, one that I knew I would remember for the rest of my life. With my arms out to the sides, eyes closed, and face tilted towards the sun, I smiled, cherishing the experience of riding Legs.

As I cruised along the beach on Legs, it was like things started clicking into place. I began to wonder if maybe Legs appeared and vanished so suddenly because he needed to go back to the ocean somehow. But then, like a tidal wave, more questions crashed into my mind. Who owned him? Was there some connection to the mermaids in all of this? Was he their pet or guardian or something?

I couldn't hold it in any longer, so I turned to Ali as we slowed down our canter to now a walk. I asked, "Dude, this is, like, raising a gazillion questions. I mean, who do you think owns Legs? Could it be the mermaids or something?"

Ali and I totally saw eye to eye on this. We both knew this was a once-in-a-lifetime, out-of-this-world experience. We were on the same wavelength about keeping it a secret. We didn't want Legs turning into some lab rat or science experiment. The thought of this secret getting out there was way too much to handle. So, we gave each other this serious nod, showing we were both super committed to guarding this mind-blowing secret. We'd treasure the time we had with Legs and keep the balance between sharing this magic and keeping it under wraps.

I couldn't help but notice that the afternoon was starting to slip through our fingers, and we'd been at the beach for what felt like forever. So, I had to remind Ali that I couldn't afford to be late again – getting grounded was not on my to-do list. We decided it was time to wrap things up, and we started gathering our stuff.

Ali mentioned she had Candy's halter in her backpack, and I could use it on Legs to lead him back to the stables. I hadn't really thought that far ahead and had to stop and mull it over for a minute. Leaving him behind wasn't even an option, and I kinda figured he'd follow us anyway. But then came the important question: how was I going to explain this to Jill at the stables?

So, I did some quick thinking and told Ali, "We can spin it that we found him just strolling around on the beach, you know? And I didn't want him to get lost or hurt, so I brought him back." It sounded pretty believable, considering the whole bizarre situation we were in. Moreover, Legs had a rep for going on his own little adventures, so it wasn't totally out there.

I thought it might be our best option. So, we used Candy's halter to lead Legs back towards the stables, walking along the shoreline. As we made our way, I couldn't help but feel the weight of the extraordinary secret we now shared.

Riding Legs, discovering his mysterious abilities, and having Ali as my partner in this bizarre experience made it all feel like an unbelievable adventure. Little did I know that more surprises and mysteries awaited us back at The Haunted Lilly.

As we made our way down the stable driveway, Jill, who was busy riding her warmblood in the arena, spotted us and called out, "Looks like you've found Legs!" I gave her a nod and said, "Yep, we stumbled upon him just wandering around near the place where we took Candy for a ride at the beach today."

Jill's chill reaction totally eased our nerves, and we took Legs back to his paddock without spilling the beans about our mind-blowing secret. As I settled Legs into his familiar spot, I couldn't resist whispering to him, "Please, dude, no more disappearing acts, okay? You totally freaked me out." I planted another gentle kiss on his nose, letting him know how thankful I was for our magical day together and how stoked I was that he seemed to choose me as his person.

Our beach day had been straight-up out-of-this-world, jam-packed with secrets, twists, and a bond that was gonna rock my world forever. As we strolled away from the stables, Ali and I exchanged these knowing looks, our shared secret locked tight between us. And then, it hit me like a ton of bricks—that pic I snapped on my cell phone last night of that painting I spotted in the hallway at The Haunted Lilly. I turned to Ali and said, "Oh you gotta check this out. I found it last night, but after today's craziness, I'm thinking it's super important."

I took out my phone and showed her the photo. Her mouth dropped open, and she exclaimed, "OMG, wow, it's crazy accurate, isn't it?"

I nodded and said, "So, we aren't the only ones that this has happened to."

It was getting pretty obvious that there was more to Port Cooper than met the eye, and secrets were just part of the deal.

I said my goodbyes to Ali and made a beeline for home before the sun called it a day. No way was I risking getting grounded. But as I cruised past Lilly, the old wooden mermaid statue by the entrance, something made me stop to check her out more closely. I couldn't help but wonder if maybe there was more to that rumour about her being named after a legit mermaid. Perhaps she even had her very own seahorse, just like I did. After all the craziness I'd seen today, I was totally convinced that anything was possible now.

When I got inside, I could hear the hushed voices of my parents coming from the kitchen. I followed the sound and found them gathered around the kitchen table with Ethan. They were all huddled together, poring over what appeared to be a super ancient book. The air in the room felt charged with something mysterious and intense.

With a tone of pride, I piped up, "Hey, guys, check it out – I'm home on time!" But instead of the excited response I expected, all I got was a half-hearted grunt from my family and a casual "That's cool." I couldn't help but feel a bit miffed. They were so engrossed in whatever they were studying that they didn't even bother to look up at me. I furrowed my brow and asked, "Okay, seriously, what's so interesting that you can't even look up for a sec?"

Ethan couldn't contain his excitement and blurted out, "Dad and I stumbled upon this super old and completely rad book inside the wall we tore down today."

My curiosity was definitely piqued now, so I wandered closer to take a peek.

My parents pushed the book closer to me, inviting me to check it out. As I got a closer look, I could see that it was filled with all sorts of mysterious symbols and writings. The whole thing had an ancient and mystical vibe to it.

Dad sidestepped to make way for me to get an even closer look at the book. He explained, "We've been studying this thing all afternoon, on and off, but none of it makes any sense. We can't figure out what language it's written in. We've been scouring Google for answers, but it's a complete and total mystery to us." The frustration in his voice was evident, and it was clear they had hit a major dead end with this book.

While I gave the book a closer look and flipped through its pages, it became pretty obvious that Dad wasn't kidding. It was written in some kind of secret code or language that was out of this world—nothing like anything I'd ever seen before. I couldn't resist muttering to myself, "This is so freaking strange.

What on earth could be inside this book that someone felt the need to stash it away in a hidden spot like a wall?"

Ethan, always the one to keep things real with his jokes, jumped in, breaking the book's mysterious aura with, "Alright, guys, enough of this mystery stuff for now. I'm absolutely starving. Feed your kid, please! I've been busting my butt all day and need food in my belly."

Mom, giving Ethan an amused look, teased him about his bottomless appetite but assured him that there was a delicious roast in the works that would soon satisfy his hunger.

Unlike Ethan, who was clearly all about the food, my mind was still racing with the book's mysteries. I told my mom, "I'm not really hungry right now. I think I need a shower to wash off all the salt and sand from my epic day at the beach."

That wasn't a complete fib; a shower was definitely in order. But, come on, I had ulterior motives—I wanted some quality time alone with that book. I scooped it up, cradling it like it was some sort of treasure, and practically sprinted up the stairs to my room. I felt a bit like Gollum and his obsession with that precious ring in "Lord of the Rings."

Santiago

CHAPTER FIVE
WHO IS SANTIAGO

I plopped down on my bed, taking a good long look at the book's cover. It had these gem things embedded in it, and the patterns and gold trim were just too cool. You could tell it was made with major care and a clear purpose. As I gently flipped through the pages, I focused on the illustrations and tried my hardest to crack the code of that mysterious text.

My heart was pounding as I turned to the next page, and then... BAM! I froze in my tracks. Right there, in a massive colourful illustration that took up the entire page, was an exact likeness of Legs, down to the tiniest detail. They even got that heart-shaped mark on his head just right. My jaw practically hit the floor.

The text below the image was a total puzzle, though. It started with "Santiago," but the rest was a blur. Santiago? Was that his name? My brain was doing gymnastics. If this book was as ancient as it looked, it meant that Legs, or Santiago, was equally old. Could he be like, a ghost seahorse or something? I was beyond baffled and seriously worn out by all the crazy discoveries.

But one thing was for sure – I had to call Ali and spill the beans on this mind-blowing revelation. She would'nt believe it!

I didn't waste a second. I whipped out my phone, snapped a quick pic of that mind-boggling page in the book with Santiago's portrait, and dialled on Ali's number like my life depended on it. When she picked up, I was practically hyperventilating with excitement and awe.

"Ali, you won't believe this! I sent you a photo, but OMG, I think I've cracked the code on Legs' real name! It's Santiago!" I could barely contain my giddy energy as I rambled on. My dad and brother found this insane ancient book today, hidden in a wall they were demolishing.

The book's written in some super weird language we can't even begin to understand. I brought it up to my room to take a closer look, and I found a page with a picture that looks exactly like Legs – I mean, down to the heart on his head."

I had to pause just to catch my breath and give my racing thoughts a moment to chill. This was some next-level, wild stuff, and I couldn't wait to hear Ali's reaction!

Ali's voice crackled with excitement through the phone, and she exclaimed, "Wow, are you kidding me? OMG, your picture just came through. WOW, it is him! Can you bring the book to the stables tomorrow? I need to see it in person."

I replied with enthusiasm, "I don't see why not. My parents think it's cool, but they don't seem that interested in it as I am. This place is just crawling with weird and the unknown, so I'm sure they're overwhelmed and busy with the renovations."

We both shared a laugh, bonding over our shared curiosity about the mysterious and magical world we were slowly uncovering in Port Cooper.

Ali had a brilliant idea. She suggested that we go back to the beach and bring Legs along, as well as the mysterious book and her mermaid shell. Maybe, just maybe, we could connect with the mermaids, or something related to them, especially if Legs had a connection like the hallway painting hinted at. It sounded both thrilling and nerve-wracking, but I agreed to meet her at the stables first and we hung up, ready for another adventure in the world of mysteries and weird surrounding Port Cooper.

I closed my cell phone from my chat with Ali and I could hear my dad calling my name, announcing that dinner was ready. As I was walking down the stairs, still in awe of the mysterious events of the day, my dad's persistent call for dinner snapped me back to reality. I realised I hadn't even had a chance to take a shower yet, as I had been engrossed in the old book and my chat with Ali. The weight of the day's revelations, from Legs' magical transformation to the enigmatic book, weighed on me.

Right before joining my family for dinner, I decided to take another look at that hallway painting. After everything I'd learned today about Legs turning into Santiago and the ancient book, I had to check it out. And guess what? The painting had totally changed! The mermaids weren't in the same spots, and now there were ghost pirates on the ship and on the land. I don't remember seeing any of that the night before. Moreover, the horse in the painting had a big, bright heart-shaped mark on its head, way more noticeable than before. It was like the painting was reacting to all the secrets and mysteries I'd uncovered today. I whipped out my phone and compared it to the pic I took last night, and sure enough, it was a whole different scene now.

"DINNER, ADDISON!" My dad's voice practically shook the house as it echoed up the stairs. I shouted down, "Yeah, yeah, Dad, I'm on my way, no need to blow a gasket!" Rushing down the stairs, I felt a sudden urge to be closer to my family, like a comforting anchor amidst all the weird stuff that had been unfolding around me.

As I stepped into the dining room, my mom shot me a worried look and immediately asked if I was alright. She mentioned that I seemed as pale as a ghost. I couldn't help but find her choice of words funny, considering Ali's story about the haunted Lilly and all the spooky legends swirling around this town.

So, I couldn't resist, and I asked my mom, "Why do we have ghosts here?" She kind of gave me this look like she wasn't expecting that question and asked, "Why would you ask that?" I took a second and then said, "You know, someone told me today that this place is famous for its ghosts, and it used to be like a magnet for ghost hunters who'd come here to hunt for 'em."

My mom totally laughed it off and replied, "Oh, that? It's just a bunch of made-up stories to get tourists excited and spend their money." She told me she grew up here and never saw any ghosts or creepy stuff, just some spiders, a snake maybe, but definitely no ghosts, nothing spooky.

I believed what my mom said, but after today, with all the magic, ghosts, and mermaids' and morphing horse stuff, it somewhat made me question everything. It was like I'd entered a whole new reality, you know? I really wanted to spill the beans and tell my mom everything, but it was just too soon. This secret was next-level crazy, and I needed time to wrap my head around it before I could talk to her or my dad and brother about it. So, for now, it remained a secret between me and Ali. Shhh!

My mom and my dad began setting the table with plates, food, and drinks as we prepared for dinner. Mom then mentioned that the paint for Lilly the wooden mermaid had arrived this afternoon, and we could start the makeover in the morning. While I had suggested the makeover, I was secretly hoping to spend the morning at the beach with Ali, Candy, and Legs. So, I asked my mom if I could help in the morning and then have the afternoon free to hang out with Ali, Candy and Legs.

She seemed surprised and asked if Legs had returned. I had to think quickly and responded, "Oh, yes, Ali and I found him wandering around on the beach today when she took us to her secret spot away from the tourists at the main beach near town."

My brother was totally into our convo and couldn't help but chuckle, "Hold up, you've got a horse named Legs? That's seriously unusual!" I went on to spill the deets about how Legs had this super mysterious arrival, popping up on the exact same day we rolled into Port Cooper, and then, like that, pulled a vanishing act for a bit, only to, magically reappear at the beach today. Since no one had a clue about his real name or where he came from, Ali started calling him Legs and it totally stuck for now. And you know what's wild? My bro actually thought it was a rad name, way cooler than some overly girly ones!

I was becoming increasingly convinced that his real name was Santiago, especially after going through the book my dad and my brother had found earlier today. However, I couldn't spill the beans with them just yet. I quickly finished dinner, helped with the clean-up, and then rushed back to my room to go over the book again. I was utterly captivated by this mysterious book, convinced that it held the answers I sought about Legs and the secrets hidden on these walls throughout the pub. It felt like I had stumbled upon a massive treasure chest just waiting to be explored with this totally cool book.

I sent a text to Ali, explaining that I had to help around here in the morning giving the big wooden mermaid a makeover, but that I could meet her at the stables after lunch. I couldn't hide my excitement and told Ali about the possibility of discovering Leg's real name and showing her the mysterious book tomorrow.

I was super pumped and totally hyped up that sleep was out of the question right now. So, I stayed up late into the night, poring over that book, desperately trying to uncover more of its secrets. The artwork in there was seriously mind-blowing, with all these crazy vibrant colours, and super intricate details. I couldn't help but wonder, you know, who was the genius behind this book and what was the important message they were trying to get across. It was a total mystery waiting to be solved!

As I gently turned page after page, I was suddenly blown away by the picture looking back at me. It was this jaw-dropping gorgeous lady with the most enchanting eyes ever, and her long, flowing blonde hair was framing her face beautifully. She was rocking this epic crown that was decked out with gems, pearls, and shells in shiny gold. And around her neck, there was a super fancy heart-shaped jewel, surrounded by all these intricate details and even more gems. She also had, like, a bazillion string pearls draped all over her neck and chest. Seriously, she looked like a total queen or, you know, someone super important!

As I read down the page, I came across the word that stopped me in my tracks: "Lilly.

Lilly? Was this talking about our mermaid friend, Lilly? Could Lilly actually be a queen? I was overwhelmed with confusion and frustration. If only I could figure out the rest of the text, maybe I could crack the code and make sense of this whole thing. Ugh, the mystery of this book was totally driving me nuts.

I was totally wiped out and lost in my thoughts, and I guess I must've drifted off to sleep at some crazy late hour. But then, out of nowhere, I got jolted awake by this super creepy sensation as if something was grabbing my leg and yanking me downward. I freaked out and jumped up in total alarm mode, scanning my room for any signs of what the heck had just touched me. But there was nothing weird in sight. So, I just froze, trying to wrap my head around it all, when out of the blue, I heard this mega loud whisper, "Give me the book." It was crystal clear, as if someone was right there in the room with me.

I hesitated for a second, then finally blurted out, "Hello? Who's there?"

Then, out of the blue, a smoky figure just materialised right in front of me—a pirate. It was a real-life pirate, staring straight at me. I was totally speechless, frozen in complete shock.

I was looking at a ghostly pirate here! He repeated his demand, "Give me the book."

I glanced over at my bed, where the book was just lying next to me. But I wasn't about to give in, no way. So, I grabbed it and held onto it like my life depended on it, and I snapped back at him all defiant, "No, you can't have it. NOW get out of my room!"

The ghostly dude started getting all up in my space, gliding over to me like smoke waving in the wind. His voice got even louder, and he straight-up yelled, "GIVE ME THE BOOK NOW!"

I was totally scared, but I stuck to my guns and told him, "No way, I won't give it to you!" Then, in this horrifying moment, I shut my eyes as he got closer and closer to me. I could feel this crazy rush of air on my face, through my hair, and then this electric zap. I freaked out and screamed at the top of my lungs. But when I finally opened my eyes, he was gone.

I was left totally shaken and completely bewildered, clutching that book tightly in my hands. Then, out of nowhere, my dad burst into my room, looking all concerned. He asked me what was going on and if I was okay. I was still trembling and not even sure about what had just happened, so I told him it was just a nightmare. I mean, there was no way I was gonna spill the beans about the whole ghostly pirate thing; it was just way too weird and freaky. Moreover, I definitely didn't want my dad to take the book away, thinking I'd lost my marbles or something.

Dad left to go back to bed, and I was feeling totally creeped out. I decided there was no way I was sleeping alone in my room that night, not after the encounter with the ghost pirate. I grabbed my pillow, blanket, and the mysterious book, and made a beeline for my brother, Ethan's room. Since I was a little girl, I had sought comfort with Ethan whenever I had a bad dream or couldn't sleep. He had a way of calming me down, often sharing interesting stories or fun facts about music. Sometimes, he'd even play me songs he had written himself until I drifted off to sleep. Tonight, I needed his presence more than ever.

I opened his bedroom door and saw that he was actually awake. I greeted him with a sheepish, "Hey" as I entered. Ethan, a bit groggy, asked if I had been the one screaming because it had woken him up, or if he had been dreaming. I told him I had a bad dream, and when he asked me what had happened, I hesitated at first, because I thought it would sound totally ridiculous. But eventually, I spilled the beans.

"Well, it's gonna sound kinda crazy, but it was about this ghost pirate who, wanted me to give him a book. Sounds pretty silly, huh?"

Ethan immediately sat up in bed, his eyes wide with disbelief. He exclaimed, "Did he have a patch on, a red scarf on his head, with dark black dreadlocks, and gold coins in his hair on one side? And, like, gold teeth, too?"

I was totally stunned, and my eyes got all big as I responded with an emphatic, "YES, that's exactly how he looked!"

Then, Ethan went on to spill the beans. He told me it wasn't just a dream. He had run into the same exact pirate dude a couple of times before. At first, he thought it was all just a dream, but his encounters were a bit different than mine. The pirate never talked to him or asked for a book. He just showed up and gave him the meanest glare and laughed from the end of Ethan's bed.

I scooted closer to Ethan's bed, plopping down right next to him. I started spilling the beans about my own run-in with the ghost pirate, how he had grabbed my leg and yanked me down my bed, while demanding that book—the same book I was holding in my hands, the one he and dad had found earlier that day. It was so obvious there was something in that book that the pirate was after.

Ethan and I exchanged bewildered glances, wondering aloud, "What the heck is going on here?" It seemed things were just getting stranger and weirder by the day in Port Cooper.

With all the ghostly craziness and that super mysterious book, I was totally convinced it was time to let Ethan in on all the weird stuff going down around us. I had total trust in him, knowing he wouldn't spill our secrets to anyone else. Moreover, I felt like I could really use his support and his perspective in dealing with this whole crazy situation that just kept getting more and more complicated.

So, I started spilling the beans to Ethan about all the crazy stuff that went down at the beach today.

Starting with how Ali had introduced me to this awesome secluded spot, the magical seashell, and the unbelievable moment when Legs had transformed from a seahorse into a real horse. I explained how we had ridden along the shore, played in the water, and discovered the mermaid shell's unique ability to summon magical creatures from the sea.

While I was dishing out all the deets of our beach adventure, Ethan was all ears, totally tuned in, and his eyes just kept getting wider with each crazy twist in the story. When I finally wrapped it up, he stared at me in total disbelief, his mind clearly trying to process the incredible tale I'd just dropped on him.

I wrapped it up, saying, "So, Ethan, there's something super extraordinary going on here, and I'm not even sure if it's good or bad, and it's not just the ghost pirate. I need your help, dude, to unravel this whole mystery with the book and these magical beings we've stumbled upon. Are you down?"

He flashed a big grin and gave me a high five, shouting, "HELL YES!!! This is gonna be EPIC!"

Ethan and I decided that for now, it was best to keep the crazy weird events we had experienced a secret from our parents. It was just too strange and unbelievable, and we didn't want to worry them or have them think we were making things up. We both understood we needed more time to dig into all the mysteries swirling around Legs, the magical seashell, and those ghostly encounters.

I invited Ethan to come to the beach with Ali and me tomorrow, with our plan to visit the beach and explore these mysteries further, especially the book. Ethan agreed to come and suggested we needed some rest now before the sun rose. We set up a makeshift bed on the floor of Ethan's room, just like we used to when I was a little girl. We lay there, side by side, feeling the bond of siblinghood and the weight of the secrets we now shared. As we closed our eyes, the mysteries of Port Cooper swirled in our minds, and sleep finally overcame us.

It was like the shortest nap ever, and it felt like no time had passed at all when I peeked over at Ethan, still snoozing away. I quickly glanced at my watch, and it was already 7 am, time to get up. I could hear Mom and Dad chatting in their room across the hall. So, I gave Ethan a gentle nudge, letting him know it was time to rise and shine.

Ethan let out this groan and mumbled, "NOOOO, it's way too early."

I totally felt his pain and replied, "I know, I'm dead tired too, but we've got a ton of stuff to tackle today with mum and dad then we've gotta make it to the beach."

Ethan seemed to recall the events of the previous night as he abruptly sat up, asking, "We dreamt all that pirate stuff, didn't we?"

I shook my head and got up, gathering my blanket and pillow to take them back to my room. "No, it wasn't a dream. It's all real, including this book and Legs transforming from a seahorse into a horse. I saw it all with my own eyes," I said, emphasising the reality of our wild experiences.

I hollered as I left Ethan's room, "I'll catch you downstairs for breakfast soon." I had already agreed last night to help Mom with painting the mermaid this morning, and he could assist Dad, too. Once we'd fulfilled our kid duties in helping out around here, we could finally head to the beach after lunch.

Ethan, still somewhat half-asleep, grunted and said, "I'm gonna be cursing that ghost pirate all day for keeping me up."

I couldn't help but chuckle as I closed the door behind me. We all knew how much Ethan cherished his sleep. Mornings weren't exactly his thing, unlike Mom and me, who were used to early starts for horse shows.

I tossed my blanket and pillow into my room from the doorway without much concern for whether they landed on the bed or the floor. I wasn't quite ready to step inside my room, even though the sun was streaming in, making everything look perfectly safe. Not today. I had no intention of dealing with any ghostly encounters this morning. I was far too tired for that. Right now, all I needed was some food and the comfort of a ghost-free zone.

I hurried downstairs as quickly as I could, still feeling totally spooked. In the kitchen, I found Mom and Dad engaged in conversation and cooking up some delicious pancakes. They greeted me warmly and asked if I managed to get any sleep after my nightmare. I replied, "I went to Ethan's room, and we talked for a bit before falling asleep."

Right on cue, Ethan entered the kitchen as well.

He chimed in, "Yep, after all these years and even in different countries, I'm still Addison's go-to safe place, because I am a legend".

I couldn't help but laugh, "Okay, okay, so maybe I'm a bit of a scaredy-cat."

I noticed Mom seemed somewhat tired herself, so I asked, "Hey, Mom, are you okay? You look like you slept on a rock all night." Then, Ethan chimed in, asking if she had bad dreams, too.

Mom looked over at us and sighed, saying, "Yeah, I didn't really sleep well. I kept having these really awful dreams that woke me up like 4 or 5 times last night."

Her words totally grabbed my attention, and I stared at her, asking, "Was it a pirate with an eye patch, a red scarf, black dreadlocks, and gold coins on one side?"

Mom dropped her plate, and her eyes locked onto mine as she gasped, "YES, that's exactly it! How did you know?"

I replied, "Because I had the same dream, but he grabbed my leg and pulled me down my bed." Mom started to laugh at first, replying no, it was just a dream, right? but then her laughter faded, and she wasn't sounding all that sure herself.

I couldn't help but voice my growing concern, asking Mom, "Don't you find it strange that you, Ethan, and I have all DREAMT the same pirate, down to the very details of how he looked, with those gold coins in his hair on one side? That's not exactly a common dream, let alone for all three of us."

Just then, Dad sheepishly raised his hand and said, "Make that four of us. I've dreamt about him, too."

Ethan was quick to react, exclaiming, "What? You too? When? Where? What did he say to you?"

Dad replied, "He wanted me to get the book. He said, 'Find the book.' But I had no idea what book he meant."

I pointed to the book in my arms and exclaimed, "THIS BOOK! He wants this book! He tried to take it from me last night, and I told him 'NO.' Then he rushed at me, screaming 'Give me the book.' It wasn't a dream, guys, it's real."

Mom interjected, desperately trying to dismiss our concerns, saying, "No, no, stop it, it's not real. We've all just been so tired, and these are just silly dreams."

I couldn't hold back any longer, cutting her off, "Mom, stop it! It's not a dream. You know there are ghosts here, don't you? You've been hiding that from all of us. Why? Tell us why?"

My mom let out this heavy sigh and took a deep breath before saying, "Alright, everyone, take a seat, and I'll explain what I know." Her request totally stunned me because she hardly ever asked us to sit down for anything unless it was super serious, like someone had died or we were, you know, moving to Australia or something.

Ethan, Dad, and I exchanged glances, a mix of curiosity and anticipation in our eyes. We knew whatever she was about to reveal would be significant.

CHAPTER SIX
THERE ARE GHOSTS IN THIS PLACE

Mom began to share a story that had been passed down through the generations in our family. She explained that the pub had a haunted history, and as a child, she used to see these pirate ghosts. They frightened her, but her Aunt Sally had reassured her, explaining that these apparitions couldn't harm her. They were just persistent, cranky spirits searching for something they had lost, and now they roamed the town in their quest for their lost treasures.

I questioned her about the book, but she confessed that she couldn't recall any mention of a book in the stories she had been told.

Mom continued with the story, emphasising that it had been exclusively passed down from one woman in our family to the next, making sure to point out that we had a lineage of only women until Ethan came into the picture. Ethan, always the joker, couldn't resist and laughed, proudly declaring himself a legend. I quickly shushed him, reminding him that this was no time for jokes, and we needed to hear this story.

Mom's story unfolded further, describing the ancient amulet's powers. She narrated how the amulet let the mermaids shift into human form and how it was first created to keep the pirates in check and protect the ocean. Those stubborn pirates, they'd been chasing after that amulet forever, swearing that the mermaids swiped it from them and demanding it back. And the stakes were crazy high because if the pirates ever got their mitts on that amulet, they'd score not just immortality but also the power to turn into humans, giving them total control over folks forever. That'd be a world ruled by pirate spirits, and that's no joke

But here's the twist: as long as the mermaids held onto the amulet, the pirates could only temporarily take over and control people. To keep their powers going and stay on their mission, they had to dip back into the ocean every night, even if just for a quick swim, to recharge their abilities and keep their influence spreading throughout the world.

As the pirates got closer and closer to uncovering the amulet's whereabouts, the situation turned super dangerous. To keep it safe from their relentless pursuit, the queen mermaid made this tough call. She decided to leave her ocean home behind and travelled as far inland as she could to hide the amulet in a place the pirates would never stumble upon. She knew the pirates were stuck with that nightly ocean dip, and this plan gave the best shot at keeping the amulet out of their clutches.

But this decision came with a massive price tag. By ditching her ocean home and stashing the amulet, the queen mermaid was well aware she could never go back to her beloved underwater world. Instead, she'd be stuck in human form for the rest of her days. It was a major sacrifice, but one she was all in for to keep that amulet away from the pirates and her home safe.

I swear I didn't even remember breathing the whole time I was listening to Mom's jaw-dropping story. I just sat there, totally stunned and bewildered.

But it was Ethan who finally broke the silence with a loud, almost hysterical laughter. "SUREEEE, Mom, and there's gold in these walls too, right?" he joked, not quite buying into the whole mermaid and pirate story.

Mom gave Ethan this look that was a total mix of, like, not being sure and being deep in thought. She said, "You know, I'm not completely sure what's real and what's make-believe anymore. But this is the story that's been passed down through our family for ages. I used to think it was all just a fun bedtime tale, but now, with all three of us having the same dream about the pirate wanting that book, I'm starting to think there might be more to it than I ever believed or gave credit to."

I was still in a state of shock, trying to process everything I had just heard. I glanced at Dad, and his expression mirrored the bewildered look I felt on my own face. I briefly considered sharing what had happened at the beach with Legs' shapeshifting into a horse out of the ocean, but something held me back, urging me to keep my mouth shut for now. It wasn't the right time yet to share that part with them.

Dad chimed in, "Well, there must be something in that book. Let's take a closer look." I placed the book on the table and said, "I want to show you something I found last night." I turned to the page with the queen and pointed at the bottom where it said, "Lilly?" I asked, "Do you think this was the queen mermaid?"

Mom examined the page more closely and responded, "Well, according to the story, the queen mermaid was named Lilly, and this pub was named after her and it was owned by her and her husband at some point. Back then it was called 'The Local Lilly.' But as time went on, with the pirates haunting it in search of the amulet, the name changed to 'The Haunted Lilly' to attract tourists, which it did quite successfully for many years. My aunt shut everything down after my uncle's sudden passing from a massive heart attack. He loved the place and managed everything. Unfortunately, she was too heartbroken to carry on after he died, so that's when it started to fall apart"

I couldn't help but blurt out in excitement with my sudden realisation, "Hang on, so let's say all of this is true, right? What if it's written in some type of mermaid language, which is why we can't read it? Maybe we aren't meant to decode it, and only another mermaid can. That way, it's guaranteed to stay safe from the pirates or anyone allied with them."

Ethan looked intrigued as he asked, " Hang on, what? Mermaids have their own language?"

I responded, "Well, why not? They're mysterious and mystical beings, so it wouldn't be too far-fetched right?"

Dad nodded in agreement, saying, "That's a good point, and it would also explain why Google translate couldn't make sense of it. You might be onto something there, Addy".

My brother let out a nervous laugh and remarked, "What is going on here? This is all very creepy, but at the same time, it's so friggin' cool."

Mom chimed in, "You know, in all the stories that have been passed down through the family, there was never any mention of a book or a hidden book. So, it's quite clear that this wasn't known to anyone except the person who placed it in the wall." Her words made sense but so much was still unknown about this book and its connection to the mermaid's secrets or Legs. Another realisation dawned on me, and I turned to my mom in excitement, saying, "Hang on, Mom. If this pub was originally owned by Lilly and her husband, and it's only been passed down through the female lineage, wouldn't that mean we are related to the queen mermaid Lilly?"

Ethan chuckled and quipped, "Well, that would explain why you and Mom love water so much, you're both part fish."

Mom took a moment, her expression all thoughtful, and then she explained, "Well, yeah, that part is true. We are related to Lilly. But you gotta remember, she became human and lost all her mermaid magic, which means we're just regular old humans, too." She made it clear that even though there might be a family connection to the queen mermaid Lilly, we wouldn't inherit any cool mermaid abilities or traits through the generations.

However, as I soaked in what Mom was saying, I couldn't help this nagging feeling deep in my gut. It was like there was this tiny voice whispering that our situation could totally change if we got our hands on that amulet. It was like a glimmer of hope or this little spark of possibility telling me that something way more extraordinary might be in store.

Dad took charge of the situation, clapping his hands and saying, "Alright, people, this story time has been fun, but there's work to be done, and it won't get itself done. Let's get moving. Your mom and I need to go to the other town to get some supplies."

I quickly chimed in, "Yes, I'm headed to the beach with Ali this afternoon, and Ethan is coming with us." I glanced at Ethan for confirmation, and he smiled, adding, "Yes, I want to check out this cool swimming spot that Addison has been bragging about." It seemed like a perfect way to break away from the eerie atmosphere and enjoy a relaxing afternoon.

I carefully wrapped the book in a large towel and placed it inside my waterproof backpack, ready to take it with me later to show Ali the page about Santiago. I had to make sure Mom and Dad didn't notice that particular page, especially Mom, who would have recognised Legs right away with that distinctive heart shape on his head

72

THE QUEEN MERMAID, LILLY

As much as I wanted to dive deeper into the book now, I knew my priority was helping Mom sand and start painting the mermaid.

Ethan and Dad headed upstairs to get on with their tasks, while Mom and I got our stuff together and headed over to the mermaid. Finally, being alone with Mom gave me the chance to dig deeper into the story.

So, I asked her, "Why didn't you ever tell me you saw ghosts here as a kid?"

She replied, "Well, I didn't want to scare you, and to be honest, I thought maybe I'd just imagined it, you know how kids' minds can play tricks on them sometimes."

I kept going, saying, "Don't you find it strange that this ghost pirate is back and making the rounds with all of us? Maybe being here has stirred up something with the whole magical realm?" It was a question that had been eating at me ever since we found the book and that pirate showed up last night.

Mom answered, "You know, I'm really not sure anymore. This was just a fun story I grew up with, but now I'm starting to wonder what's actually real and what's not."

I couldn't hold back my excitement and blurted out, "I think it's totally awesome, and I'm actually pumped to learn more, even if it's a little creepy. It's like, the highlight of my life right now."

Mom chuckled and nodded, saying, "You're absolutely right. It's been anything but boring since we got to Port Cooper." We both shared a giggle, totally recognising how our lives had taken this unexpected and mind-boggling twist.

As we got busy with the mermaid project, we switched our chat to something else, giving us a much-needed break from all the creepiness and mystery that had been swirling around us. We chatted about horses, and Mom couldn't hide her enthusiasm for getting back in the saddle. She mentioned that Jill at the riding school had a perfect horse for her to start riding again. I could see how thrilled she was about the prospect of riding once more, and it made me super happy to know that Mom was getting back to her true passion – horses.

I totally understood that Mom and Dad had been busting their tails to bring the pub back to life and get it ready for reopening, especially with all the costs involved in the move and renovations. It was obvious they were dead set on making it a hit. But I also knew that Mom needed a break from all that hustle and bustle, and there's nothing better than escaping the daily grind and spending time around horses.

With our chores done, Ethan and I gathered our beach stuff and some snacks. I made sure to bring my backpack with the book safely wrapped up. We headed over to the stables to meet Ali and get Legs and Candy. During the walk, Ethan and I kept up our convo about the book and all the weird stuff happening around us. He was genuinely pumped and totally into the idea of going on an adventure, just like me.

I shared with him that I wasn't quite ready to spill the beans to Mom and Dad about how Legs had shape-shifted. Ethan nodded in agreement, thinking it might worry them, especially with me riding him and all. It felt somewhat strange to talk about it out loud, but deep down, I knew Legs wouldn't do anything to hurt me. There was this special connection between us, and it felt like our matching hearts somehow linked us in a way that defied explanation.

When we got to the stables, Ali was already there, all set with Candy and even had a spare bridle for me to use on Legs for the day. I realised that Ali hadn't met Ethan yet, so I introduced them. From the sheepish smile on Ali's face and the starry-eyed look she gave my brother, it was clear she found him cute. I couldn't help but roll my eyes; though it wasn't the first time I'd seen that kind of reaction from girls meeting my brother. I guess he's sort of cute, but to me, he's just my dorky brother.

As we made our way to the front of the stables to get Legs, I whispered quietly to Ali that I had spilled the beans to Ethan about Legs' fancy party trick from yesterday afternoon. She looked a bit worried, but I quickly reassured her that Ethan was totally trustworthy and would keep our secret safe.

I opened the gate and entered Legs' paddock. Just like before, he came straight to me and lowered his head, allowing me to put the bridle on. I wasn't certain if he had ever had a bit in his mouth before, but judging by his reaction, it seemed likely.

I patted him and hopped on bareback. (For those reading who might not know much about horse equipment, a horse bit is a part of the bridle and its made from stainless steel or copper that goes in a horse's mouth and is used to help guide and control the horse's direction, similar to a steering wheel in a car).

Ethan decided to walk alongside us, showing no interest in getting on a horse or trying out the double ride, as he had always been a bit nervous around horses and it just wasn't his thing. While we rode towards the secluded beach, I filled Ali in on all the spooky ghost pirate stuff, explaining how they had visited not only me and Ethan but also my parents. She was totally shocked, but her excitement matched ours as we talked about all these mysterious happenings.

We reached the secluded part of the beach and laid out our things. I was eager to show Ali the pages about Legs that I had discovered the previous night. I carefully pulled the book from my backpack and unwrapped it. We all sat down on our towels, and I found the page I had been hiding from my parents.

Excitedly, I pointed at the picture and exclaimed, "LOOK, it's Legs!" We all gazed at the picture and then back at Legs. Ali was astonished and said, "OMG, you're right, it is him. Exactly the same."

I then revealed, "His name is Santiago." I called out to Legs, "Hey Santiago!" He pricked up his ears and turned to look at us. It was as if he recognised his name. We all marvelled at the realisation that this was his true name all along. So, no more calling him Legs; his name was Santiago.

I expressed my frustration to Ali, "I wish we could make out the rest of the text in the book to see what it says about Santiago and learn more about him. I think the book is written in some type of secret mermaid language to keep its contents safe from getting into the wrong hands, like the ghost pirates."

Ali nodded and chimed in, "Yeah, this is like nothing I've ever seen before. Well, at least we know Santiago came out of the ocean and turned into a horse." We both shared a little giggle, finding some relief in the sheer craziness of the situation. "Yeah," I agreed, "we definitely do." The enigmas surrounding Santiago and the book just kept getting more fascinating and complicated by the minute.

Ethan tossed out a question, saying, "So, if we go by the age of the book, that means Santiago is very old too. I guess magical creatures are immortal?" Ali and I exchanged uncertain glances and then shrugged. I replied, "I guess so. All of this is new to me, to us." It was a pretty mind-boggling thought, and we were still trying to wrap our heads around all the mysteries tied to Santiago and the magical world he seemed to be a part of.

I got up and approached Santiago, patting him affectionately. I whispered to him, "I'm so happy to meet you, Santiago. What other secrets do you have, beautiful boy?" I kissed him gently and then removed his bridle. It was time for us to have some fun and go for a ride. I hopped onto Santiago's back, and we cantered off along the beach, just as we had done the day before.

I could tell Santiago was enjoying it as much as I was. As we rode along the shoreline, I could hear Ali shouting from behind us, "WAIT FOR US!!!"

I laughed and called back, "Hurry up, slow coach!" It was another Australian slang word for hurry up. I was getting used to all these funny slang words I had picked up in my short time here.

Finally, Ali and Candy had caught up to me and Santiago. We stopped, turned around, and began heading back to our belongings and where Ethan was. I could see Ethan was now at the shoreline, getting into the ocean.

Ali suggested, "Let's go back and take the horses into the water with Ethan."

I was excited about the idea and replied, "Yes, that will be awesome. We didn't get to do that yesterday with all the excitement of Santiago's morphing out of the ocean trick." It sounded like a perfect way to enjoy the day at the beach.

We cantered back along the shoreline and slowed down as we approached Ethan. Ali and I were giggling, and I couldn't help but feel an overwhelming sense of happiness. Riding Santiago, being with my new best friend, Ali, and sharing these moments with my brother, Ethan, made me truly appreciate my new life in Australia. Despite the seriously creepy and mysterious events unfolding around us, I couldn't deny that I was loving every moment of this new adventure.

CHAPTER SEVEN
OMG, IM A MERMAID!

W e reached Ethan on the shoreline, still laughing as we enjoyed the water splashing up on us. Ali started to ride Candy into the waves, going out deeper and deeper. I followed her on Santiago. Ali said to me, "What if Santiago morphs back into a seahorse?" I laughed and said, "I guess I will hang on and ride a seahorse". We both laughed and kept going deeper until our legs where now deep in the ocean.

All of a sudden, a tingling sensation started creeping over my legs, starting off slow but quickly intensifying. Fear gripped me. Was something grabbing me? I glanced down at my legs in shock, and I couldn't believe my eyes as they underwent a dramatic transformation. Panic surged through me, and I screamed out to Ethan and Ali, "Guys, something's happening to my legs! They feel so weird!"

My legs were changing even faster now, and I began to slide off Santiago's back. Ethan hurried to my side, clear concern in his eyes, and Ali did her best to join us on Candy as quickly as possible. I kept exclaiming, "OMG, guys, I can't feel my legs, they're not working!" In desperation, I reached my hands into the water to feel my legs, only to discover that I no longer had legs. Instead, I had a massive FIN!!!

I was still in complete disbelief, struggling to wrap my head around the incredible transformation that had just occurred. Ali, right beside me on Candy, let out a shocked scream and stammered as she tried to get the words out, "Addison, you're, you're, you're a MERMAID!"

Ethan looked down and suddenly exclaimed, "Addison, you have a fin! OMG, YOU ARE A MERMAID!"

I gazed down at myself and realised they were absolutely right. I had indeed become a mermaid. I tried to move my new fin, which had just been my legs a few minutes ago. The fin created a massive splash in the water. It felt incredibly powerful.

Ali and Ethan both continued to stare at me in shock, struggling to grasp the unbelievable sight in front of them. Finally, Ethan broke the silence with a wide-eyed, "Wow, my sister is a mermaid."

Panic gripped me as I screamed out, "OMG, I'M A MERMAID!"

The shock and confusion were overwhelming. I couldn't understand how this transformation had happened, and I desperately wanted answers to the impossible questions racing through my mind.

Ethan raised a practical concern, "How are we going to get you home? We're going to have to tell Mum and Dad about this. I don't think we can hide that fin under a dress, right?" He started to chuckle, but I was too overwhelmed to find any humour in the situation.

I retorted, "This is really no time to be joking, Ethan. I just turned into a mermaid." I pointed at my fin while giving him a stern look.

Ali quickly responded, "Didn't you say you thought the book was written in some type of mermaid language? Now that you're a mermaid, maybe you can read it. Maybe there's an answer in there for why you're now a mermaid and if you can change back."

"That's a great idea," I said. "Ethan, can you pick me up and take me back to the book?" The book was sitting on our towels on the beach. Ethan put his arms under me and lifted me up to carry me to shore, commenting, "You're still heavy as a stone, Addy."

I replied, "Well, yes, I imagine my huge fin has something to do with that." Ali followed Ethan, and Santiago was right next to me the whole time, now following Ethan as he carried me back to land. There was something about being with him, riding him, that seemed connected to this incredible transformation and also gave me comfort that I knew it would all be OK.

Ethan gently sat me down on my towel, and Ali hopped off Candy, sitting down next to me. She marvelled at my new mermaid fin, and I couldn't help but agree with them—it was truly beautiful, with its vibrant shades of blues, aqua, with hints of purple and pink. Ali excitedly urged me to move it, and I wiggled the end of my fin, like I would wiggle my toes causing it to move up and down in a graceful motion. Ali couldn't contain her enthusiasm as she exclaimed, "WOW, this is just way too cool. My best friend is a real-life mermaid."

As Ali and I admired my newfound mermaid fin, Ethan grabbed the book and handed it to me. I took the book and opened it to a random page. To my amazement, the text on the page appeared to be magically written in English. I exclaimed with astonishment, "Guys, I can read it! It's like it's all in English now. I was right; it was in code to protect it." The revelation left us all in awe, and I couldn't wait to read more and uncover the secrets hidden within the book.

My major concern right now was understanding how I had become a mermaid and whether there was a way to reverse the transformation. I wasn't ready to give up my life on land as a 14-year-old teenager, and the prospect of being a mermaid brought with it a multitude of questions and uncertainties.

As I scanned through the book, desperately searching for any information about humans turning into mermaids, I grew increasingly frustrated. Page after page revealed nothing about my current situation. The book did mention that mermaids had the ability to turn into humans, but only if they possessed the amulet.

Ali suggested that I go to the page about Santiago, and I followed her advice. The passage described Santiago as a seahorse with the power to transform into a horse, but again, it mentioned that this transformation required the amulet. We didn't have the amulet, so how had Santiago and I managed to transform without it? The answers remained hidden, and my frustration grew until I finally closed the book, feeling a bit defeated not finding the answers I needed right now.

Ethan's suggestion of carrying me home and covering my tail in towels was sweet, but it just wouldn't work. I could still imagine my mermaid tail peeking out, and that was definitely a no-go. The last thing I wanted was to end up as some sort of lab experiment. We needed to figure out a better plan that would let me keep my newfound condition under wraps.

Ali came up with an interesting idea. She suggested, "Hey, why don't you go back into the ocean and get on Santiago? I mean, you were riding him when all of this mermaid stuff happened, right?

Maybe he's the key to all of this, kind of like the amulet." It sounded crazy, but at that point, we were willing to try anything to figure out how to change me back into a human.

Ali's suggestion made sense. Since Santiago had transformed from a seahorse to a horse without the amulet, maybe he held the key to reversing my transformation. We shared a connection, evidenced by the matching love hearts, so it was worth trying. As Ethan carried me back to the ocean and let me go in the water, I felt my fin growing stronger, and the sudden urge to swim overcame me.

I told Ethan and Ali who were standing together looking at me that I wanted to have a quick swim to test out my new fin's before attempting to ride Santiago out of the ocean. They agreed, and I swam off, discovering that I could move through the water with incredible speed and grace.

I had swum so far out that the shoreline was barely visible when I suddenly heard a soft voice saying my name, "Hello, Addison." I instantly spun around to find two beautiful mermaids with the most amazing kind green eyes looking at me.

One introduced herself as Luna, and the other as Freya. They reassured me that they were here to help. Overwhelmed by this unexpected encounter, I responded with a simple, "Hello," but then I couldn't help but wonder how they knew my name. So, I asked them.

Luna smiled and responded, "Santiago." It all started to make sense. I knew Santiago must be connected to the mermaids, especially with his shape-shifting abilities.

Luna was the leader of the mermaid duo, and she shared some intriguing family history.. Apparently, I've got mermaid royalty running through my veins, going way back to my great-great-great-great-great-great grandmother who was, you guessed it, a queen. So, our family moving to Port Cooper got the ghost pirates all riled up, making them hunt harder for the amulet.

Now here's the twist: Santiago and I transforming without the amulet? Nobody knows how that's even possible. Luna thinks it might be linked with our family bloodline and those cute matching love hearts we've got going on. But seriously, it's never happened before, so they're just as baffled as we are.

But wait, there's more drama to it! The pirates had to dip back into the ocean every night to recharge their powers, but that was totally trashing the ocean and killing all the underwater Sealife. Freya alerted us to the importance of finding the amulet before the pirates do. She emphasised, "We've gotta find that amulet before the pirates score it. If they succeed, they'll gain immortality and dominate humans, causing significant chaos in both of our worlds."

Freya shared some seriously spooky stuff that sent chills down my spine. She cautioned, "Addison, never swim out this far by yourself. We always roll in pairs for a reason. There's some deep-sea weirdness you don't wanna mess with, trust me." It was like a scene out of a scary movie, and I was freaked out.

I was genuinely shaken now. Not only had I recently transformed into a mermaid (seriously, what's going on?), but I was also engaged in a conversation with mermaids in the middle of the ocean, and they were entrusting me with the responsibility of saving the world from ghostly pirates? And the rule about not swimming alone? And then, before I could even ask Luna or Freya a zillion questions or say goodbye, they pulled a vanishing act. So, there I was, trying to wrap my head around this cray-cray info dump.

I swam back to the shore as fast as I could, thoroughly spooked, where Ethan, Ali, Candy, and Santiago were all waiting for me. Their faces were a total mix of relief and excitement when they saw me. I could tell they were dying to know what had happened, but I was like, "Hold on, hold on! Let's make sure our plan works first. I'll spill all the deets on our way home, I promise!" I just wanted to get out of the ocean as fast I could.

Time was ticking, and we needed to hustle to get back home before it got too late and I faced serious grounding for the rest of my life. I called Santiago over, coaxing him a bit deeper into the water so I could sit on him all Ariel-style with my shiny new fin. I gripped his mane, closed my

MERMAID LUNA

eyes, and whispered, "Come on, Santiago, pretty, please let this work." I could feel him making his way toward the shore, and then, out of the blue, that same tingly feeling hit me again. I looked down, and BOOM, my legs were morphing back! I couldn't contain my excitement, so I shouted to Ali and Ethan, "OMG, IT'S WORKING! MY LEGS ARE BACK!" I was practically screaming, "YAHOO!" while fist punching the air in excitement. I was definitely not ready to be a full-time mermaid.

I rode Santiago up to our towels and bags and hopped off, patting my legs, "Wait, did I just dream that whole mermaid thing?" I've seriously never been so psyched to see my legs.

Ali and Ethan were like, "Nope, no dream, it totally happened!" It was wild, and I couldn't wait to tell them all the juicy details on the way back home about what Luna and fay Freya had told me.

After wrapping up the mysterious book and stashing it safely in my backpack, Ethan and Ali started packing their stuff as we prepared to head home. Now that I had my legs back, I found myself appreciating them like never before.

As we walked home, I couldn't wait to spill the beans about my epic mermaid adventure and meeting Luna and Freya. I filled them in on the warning they shared with me, the whole deal about Santiago and me having some kind of special power, and the urgent mission to stop those pesky pirates from getting their hands on the amulet. They were both in shock but brimming with excitement about it at the same time.

Ethan, being the responsible older brother, suggested, "I think it's time we spill the beans to Mom and Dad. They already know about the ghost pirates, so it's better they hear everything."

I wanted to tell them too, but I was worried they'd overreact and say, "No more Santiago!" That would be a real bummer.

MERMAID FREYA

Ethan gave me a reassuring look and said, "I don't think they will. Santiago is part of this, and you need him. You know our parents, they're pretty cool, and we don't need to hide things from them, especially something like this. It's way above our pay grade here, sis."

Ali nodded in agreement and added, "You know, you should definitely tell them everything. It's making me rethink all those stories my dad used to tell me, and now they seem more real than ever. If something is out there attacking boats, it's a real threat."

I had completely forgotten about the boat attack detail while I was out in the ocean. I was glad I didn't remember it at the time; otherwise, I might have freaked out and had a panic attack and drowned. It also made me wonder if there was a connection between the boat attacks and Freya's warning about not swimming too far out alone.

Ali suddenly remembered the mermaid seashell. "Hey, I bet you could use the mermaid cell phone to call Luna and Freya now that you're a mermaid," she suggested.

I thought for a moment and replied, "Good point, but let's just get home and figure it all out later. It's just too overwhelming to think about all at once."

So, we got the horses back to the stables and then headed home. After saying our goodbyes to Ali, she went towards the pier, and both Ethan and me went the other way, heading back to The Haunted Lilly.

Walking in silence gave us both a chance to process everything that had just happened that afternoon. I knew Ethan must be trying to make sense of it all, just like me. It was truly mind-boggling how much my life had changed in the short few weeks since we arrived in Port Cooper. I was now a mermaid, or at least part mermaid. I couldn't help but wonder if that made me a kind of "part-bred" mermaid like a part bred horse.

We arrived at the entrance of The Haunted Lilly, and there stood the wooden mermaid, Lilly. I stopped, clutching my backpack tightly against my chest with the mysterious book safely inside. I gazed at the statue with a whole new perspective now, knowing that we were truly related.

As I stood there, I couldn't help but wonder how to begin the conversation with my parents. Just then, Ethan opened the front door and turned to me, encouraging me to follow him. I nodded and walked in beside him. My heart was racing so hard that I thought it might leap out of my chest. My palms grew sweaty, and I felt a bit lightheaded.

Ethan reassured me that I wasn't alone, and it was not the time to back out. Mom and Dad greeted us in the dining room, and Mom asked how our afternoon at the beach had been. Ethan exchanged a knowing look with me, and I took a deep breath, glancing back at him as he nodded in support. I said, "Mom, Dad, I have something very important to tell you."

With that, I retrieved the book from my backpack and placed it carefully on the table. Opening it to the page featuring Santiago's illustration, I pushed the book closer to Mom and Dad for them to see. Mom's eyes widened as she recognised the image of "Legs," and she uttered his name, "Santiago," as if she were asking me a question.

Both Ethan and I took our seats, and I began, "What I'm about to tell you is going to change everything."

TO BE CONTINUED...

Book two coming soon.

I'm sorry to leave you hanging here, but as I mentioned earlier, there's just too much to fit into one book. More stories are coming, and I'm looking forward to sharing more of Santiago's incredible adventures with you.

See you all soon

Addison Steel

86

ADDISON WITH SANTIAGO

Amurath Santiago and
some of his prestigious
American wins
with riders Elise Crisafulli
and Ashley Price

Scottsdale Arabian Horse Show
Unanimous Champion
Scottsdale, Arizona | February 2009

Photos by Osteen | Schatzberg | Stine | Kerri Hill

Candy

DIAMOND ROAD CANDY CRUSH

Candy's first show with me as her
wner winning Champion
Partbred Arabian. Shown by her
halter trainer Damien Henricus.

Candy is about to start her
saddle career very soon!

EXPLORE OUR WEBSITE TO DISCOVER EXCITING NEW DETAILS ABOUT
THE UPCOMING BOOK INSTALLMENTS AND THE TV SHOW COMING SOON.

WWW.SANTIAGOENTERTAINMENT.COM.AU

SEE YOU REAL SOON MATEY

www.ingramcontent.com/pod-product-compliance
Lightning Source LLC
Chambersburg PA
CBHW071142250626
47159CB00006B/2266